I Am Not Your Friend I Am Your Mother

Rene' Stanley

BOOKS by RENE

Rene' Stanley

ISBN: 979-8-9922952-2-1 (paperback)

Library of Congress Control Number:

Cover Design by Rene' Stanley

booksbyrene@renehome.net

www.books-by-rene.store

To the most precious creation of God
To my mother, who showed me that strength and tenderness are not opposites but partners in the dance of motherhood. Your unwavering faith and quiet determination laid the foundation for everything I am today.
And to the remarkable circle of women who surrounded her - my aunts, godmothers, and church mothers - your collective wisdom formed a tapestry of love, faith, and resilience that has blessed generations. Through Sunday dinners, late-night phone calls, and countless prayers, you demonstrated what it truly means to raise children in faith. Your stories, sacrifices, and steadfast devotion to family and God continue to echo through time. This book is a testament to your legacy - a legacy built not on worldly success but on the eternal principles you held dear. May your example continue to inspire mothers for generations to come.
With deep gratitude and love,
Rene'

To Reverend Marcus Bowles, III,
Your words have been a beacon of light, and your sermons have provided me with profound inspiration and guidance. Through your teachings that I write this book. Thank you for your dedication to spreading hope and love.
With heartfelt gratitude,
Rene' Stanley

Contents

Chapter 1

Introduction

I stood in the kitchen, arms crossed and eyes fixed on Michael. The remnants of an unfinished homework assignment lay scattered on the table, mingling with candy wrappers he wasn't supposed to have. His head hung low, but defiance still sparkled in his eyes.

"Michael," I began, my voice steady but firm, "we've talked about this before. Why did you sneak those candies into your room? You know the rules."

"It's just candy, Mom. It's not a big deal." He shifted his weight from one foot to the other, unwilling to meet my gaze.

"It's not just about the candy," I said, stepping closer. "It's about obedience and respect. When you break these small rules, you're showing a lack of both."

He scoffed, his frustration bubbling over. "You're always on my case! You're not my friend!"

I paused for a moment, letting his words hang in the air. My heart ached at the rift between us, but I couldn't let it deter me from what I knew was right.

"You're right," I replied, my tone unwavering. "I'm not your friend. I'm your mother."

Michael's eyes widened slightly at my resolute response, but he quickly masked it with a scowl.

"And as your mother," I continued, "it's my responsibility to guide you, even when it's hard and even when you don't like it."

He kicked at an imaginary spot on the floor, frustration radiating off him. "Why can't you just let me be? I'm not a little kid anymore."

I took a deep breath, praying silently for wisdom and patience. "Being older doesn't mean you're exempt from consequences or responsibilities. God entrusts parents with the task of raising their children in His ways."

Michael's face softened just a fraction at the mention of God. We'd had many talks about faith and responsibility before; he knew where I stood.

"I do this because I love you," I added gently but firmly. "And because it's my duty to help you grow into a man who honors God and respects others."

He said nothing, staring down at his feet again. Silence stretched between us, thick and heavy.

Finally, he looked up, eyes searching mine for something—understanding perhaps or even just a sign that this sternness came from love.

"We'll talk more about this later," I said quietly but firmly. "Right now, clean up this mess and finish your homework."

As Michael turned to clean up his mess, I paused, the weight of my words settling over me like a heavy cloak. "I'm not your friend. I'm your mother." It echoed in my mind, and I couldn't help but reflect quietly on the gravity of that statement.

In today's world, popular culture seems to push parents to be casual friends with their children. It tells us to be their buddies, to let them navigate life with minimal guidance. But deep in my heart, I have always believed my role as a Christian mother demands much more than that.

I thought back to Proverbs 22:6: "Train up a child in the way he should go: and when he is old, he will not depart from it." My parents had taken that verse seriously, and they had instilled it in me with every lesson and every prayer. They were stern at times, yes, but always out of love and a desire to see me grow into a woman who walked with God.

Michael's defiance reminded me so much of my younger self—stubborn and resistant to authority. But I also remembered the countless prayers my mother had whispered for me, the sleepless nights spent worrying about my choices. Now it was my turn.

I watched Jacob pick up his scattered papers and crumpled candy wrappers, his movements slow and deliberate. My heart ached for him; I knew he didn't understand yet why I had to be firm, why I couldn't just be his friend.

The world told him that parents should be lenient, that they should indulge their children's whims to keep them happy. But happiness built on a foundation of indulgence and leniency would crumble under the weight of life's real challenges.

No, my calling as a mother was much higher. It required me to stand firm in my convictions, even when it made me unpopular in his eyes. It meant guiding him through the narrow path that led to life, as Jesus spoke of in Matthew 7:14.

As I continued to watch Michael work silently, I sent up another prayer—one among many—for wisdom and strength. For the ability to balance love with discipline, mercy with justice.

"Michael," I called softly.

He looked up from his task, surprise flickering across his face at the gentleness in my voice.

"I love you," I said simply.

He nodded slowly before returning to his work. In that small gesture, I saw a glimmer of understanding begin to take root. And though the road ahead would be long and fraught with challenges, I knew that with God's guidance, we would walk it together.

I took a deep breath, my mind racing with thoughts of how best to convey the importance of what I was trying to do. Raising children requires tough love, not friendship. It's a truth I've clung to, even when society's permissive views threatened to sway me.

"Michael," I began, my voice steady but firm, "there are times when being your mother means making hard choices. Choices that might not make sense to you right now."

He looked at me, curiosity mixed with frustration in his eyes.

"I'm not here to be your friend," I continued. "Friends come and go. They tell you what you want to hear. But as your mother, my role is different. My responsibility is to guide you, even if that means being the bad guy sometimes."

Michael's face hardened, but I pressed on.

"The Bible calls us to raise our children with discipline and instruction," I said. "Ephesians 6:4 tells fathers not to provoke their children to anger but to bring them up in the discipline and instruction of the Lord. It applies to mothers too."

He fidgeted with a pencil, clearly wanting this conversation to end.

"Permissiveness might seem like love," I said gently, "but true love often means setting boundaries and enforcing rules. It means preparing you for the world outside this home—a world that isn't always kind or forgiving."

Jacob sighed, his shoulders slumping slightly.

"I know it's hard," I said softly, feeling a pang of sympathy for him. "But you'll understand one day why it's necessary."

He looked down at his hands, silent but listening.

"I want you to grow into a man who respects others and walks in God's ways," I added. "That's why we have these rules. They're not just for show; they're meant to shape your character."

The room grew quiet as he absorbed my words.

"This isn't an easy path," I admitted, more to myself than him. "It's a difficult battle, but one that must be waged."

Michael met my eyes then, and for a brief moment, I saw a flicker of comprehension. He didn't say anything—he didn't need to—but the silence between us spoke volumes.

I stood there for a moment longer before stepping back, allowing him space to process what had been said.

I stood there, giving Jacob the space he needed, my thoughts drifting back to the foundations of our family. My husband John and I had built a life together in a modest suburban home, tucked away in a quiet neighborhood. John worked as an engineer, his steady hands and meticulous mind shaping not just machines but the stability of our household. We had three children: Michael, our headstrong teenager; Jessica, the middle child with a heart for art and music; and little Ethan, who at eight was already showing signs of a curious mind.

Our family attended Grace Community Church every Sunday without fail. Pastor Williams's sermons often served as the anchor points for our week, grounding us in Scripture and reinforcing the values we strived to live by. Our church wasn't just a place of worship; it was our extended family, a community that shared our beliefs and supported us through thick and thin.

But despite the traditional veneer of our suburban life, our parenting style often set us apart. John and I believed that raising children required more than just love and affection—it required structure, discipline, and a firm adherence to biblical principles. This countercultural approach wasn't always easy to maintain in a world that seemed to champion permissiveness and instant gratification.

John's support made all the difference. While he might have been more lenient at times, his unwavering faith and wisdom provided a balance that kept our family grounded. Together, we navigated the challenges of parenting with prayerful consideration, always seeking God's guidance.

I thought back to how we handled each of our children's unique personalities. Jessica's creative spirit often led her into daydreams that needed gentle redirection. Ethan's boundless curiosity required constant vigilance to ensure he stayed safe while exploring the world around him. And Michael—well, Michael tested boundaries more than either of his siblings ever did.

The world outside might have looked at us as strict or old-fashioned, but within the walls of our home, we knew we were forging something far more valuable: character molded by faith and integrity. As I returned my focus to Michael, still sitting there with that pencil in his hand, I felt a renewed sense of purpose.

This journey we were on wasn't easy—parenting never is—but it was one worth every effort we poured into it.

Looking back over the last twenty years, raising Michael, Jessica, and Ethan was like traversing a winding, often treacherous path. Each step demanded faith, patience, and an unwavering commitment to the principles John and I held dear. This isn't just a reflection; it's a memoir of a journey steeped in trials and tests of faith.

I remember vividly the nights spent on my knees, praying for wisdom as we faced the challenges each child brought to our doorstep. Jessica's gentle spirit was a balm in many ways but also required careful nurturing to ensure she didn't lose herself in her art. Ethan's insatiable curiosity led to many a scraped knee and broken vase, yet his thirst for knowledge always brought a smile to my face. And Michael—oh, Michael—his rebellious streak often tested the very limits of my resolve.

But even amidst these struggles, there were moments of pure grace that reminded me why this journey was worth every hardship. The first time Jacob stood up in church to recite a Bible verse he'd memorized, the joy on Emily's face when she played her first solo at a church recital, Ben's endless questions about creation during family devotionals—all these moments stitched together a tapestry of faith that defined our family.

Society often pushed back against our methods. Friends would question why we didn't allow certain freedoms or why we insisted on such strict adherence to biblical standards. But John and I knew that our role as parents wasn't to be liked; it was to guide our children toward a deeper understanding of their faith and moral responsibility.

There were times I doubted myself—wondered if the strictness was too much or if the battles were too fierce. Yet every time doubt crept in, I found solace in Scripture and in John's unwavering support. We reminded ourselves that God entrusted us with these three souls, and it was our duty to shepherd them faithfully.

As I look back now, I see not just the struggles but the growth that came from them. Our children didn't just learn obedience; they learned integrity, compassion, and an unshakeable faith. The seeds we planted through discipline and love took root in ways I could never have imagined.

These twenty years taught me that parenting is less about perfection and more about perseverance. The trials were many, but each one forged stronger bonds within our family and deeper roots in our faith. And for that, I remain eternally grateful.

This is the story of how, by God's grace, we aimed to mold souls, not make friends. As a mother, my highest calling was not to win a popularity contest but to shape the character of Michael, Jessica, Emily and Ethan. This philosophy often placed me at odds with them, especially during their teenage years.

I remember one evening vividly. Michael had just stormed out of the room after another heated argument. He yelled back at me, "You're not my friend!" The sting of his words hung in the air, but I stood firm.

"You're right," I called after him. "I'm not your friend. I'm your mother."

In those moments of tension and rebellion, it would have been easier to relent, to give in to the desire for peace and friendship. But I knew my role demanded more. Being a spiritual mother figure meant guiding them with a steady hand, even when it led us through storms.

Popular culture often urged parents to be casual friends with their kids, but I couldn't subscribe to that notion. Friendship could wait; what they needed now was a mother willing to stand firm in her convictions. A mother who loved them enough to say 'no' when it was necessary, who cared enough to set boundaries grounded in biblical truths.

There were countless nights when John and I sat together at the kitchen table, discussing how best to navigate this countercultural approach to parenting. John's unwavering support was my anchor. His role as the family's provider extended beyond his job at the engineering firm; he provided emotional and spiritual stability that we all leaned on.

We both believed our suburban home wasn't just a place of shelter but a training ground for life's greater battles. Our church community supported us in this mission. Pastor Daniels often reminded us during Sunday sermons that parenting is a divine responsibility—a stewardship entrusted by God Himself.

Yes, there were moments when I felt militantly unpopular with my own children. Times when Emily would retreat into her room, shutting out the world—and me—with her art supplies strewn around her like a fortress. Times when Ben's endless questions turned into frustrated silence because he didn't like the answers rooted in Scripture.

But those were the moments that defined our journey. They taught me that molding souls required a love far deeper than friendship—a love willing to endure misunderstanding and resentment for the sake of eternal truths.

In looking back over these years, I see how each act of tough love was an investment in their future character and faith. And through it all, God's grace was our guide, sustaining us through every challenge and triumph.

One memory, more than any other, still brings a lump to my throat. Jessica was only five, her wide eyes full of innocent curiosity and a hint of confusion. She stood in the living room, clutching his favorite stuffed rabbit, its ears worn from countless hugs.

"Mommy, why can't I go to Tiffany's party?" she asked, her voice trembling. "Don't you love me?"

Her question struck me like a blow. The easy answer would have been to give in, to let her join the other children at the party. But this was one of those moments that demanded more.

I knelt down to her level, brushing a stray lock of hair from her face. "Jess," I began, choosing my words carefully, "I love you more than anything in this world."

She looked up at me, her eyes searching for understanding. "Then why can't I go?"

I took a deep breath, feeling the weight of what I had to explain. "Because sometimes loving someone means making hard choices. Choices that keep them safe and help them grow."

Her little brow furrowed in confusion. "But it's just a party."

I nodded, understanding her perspective but knowing she couldn't grasp the bigger picture yet. "Yes, it is just a party. But there are things there that aren't good for you, things that could hurt you even if they seem fun right now."

She looked down at his rabbit, stroking its worn ear thoughtfully. "Like what?"

"Like some of the games they play," I explained gently. "Or the shows they watch there." I paused, searching for a way to make it clearer for her young mind. "Imagine if you ate too much candy all at once. It might taste good at first, but then you'd get a tummy ache."

Her eyes widened as he nodded slowly.

"I don't want you to have a 'tummy ache' in your heart or your mind," I continued. "So sometimes I have to say no because I love you so much."

Jessica's face softened as she absorbed my words. She didn't fully understand yet, but she trusted me enough to accept it for now.

She reached out and wrapped her tiny arms around my neck in a hug that spoke volumes more than words ever could.

In that moment, I realized just how deeply my love for my children ran—enough to make those tough calls and endure their temporary disappointment for their long-term well-being.

And as Jessica clung to me, seeking comfort in my embrace, I whispered a silent prayer for strength and wisdom to continue guiding them with love grounded in faith and truth.

Chapter 2

Laying the Foundations

T he sun barely peeked over the horizon as I cracked eggs into a sizzling pan. The familiar sound of bacon popping in the skillet mingled with the sleepy grumbles coming from upstairs. It was a typical weekday morning, the house teetering on the edge of chaos as we tried to get everyone up, dressed, and fed before school.

"Mom! Where's my other sock?" Jessica called from her bedroom. She was our middle child, always losing something at the last minute.

"In your drawer, where it belongs!" I called back, flipping the bacon with practiced ease. "Remember to check your top drawer."

John shuffled into the kitchen, his tie askew and eyes still heavy with sleep. He kissed my cheek and reached for a cup of coffee. "Morning," he murmured, his voice a gravelly whisper.

"Morning," I replied, handing him a plate of toast. "Can you check on Ethan? He's been hitting snooze for the past twenty minutes."

John nodded and headed back up the stairs. Moments later, I heard him knocking on Ethan's door, coaxing him out of bed with promises of pancakes.

"Sarah," Jessica whined from her spot at the kitchen table, her middle sibling trying to finish her homework while nibbling on a piece of toast. "I don't understand this math problem."

I set down my spatula and moved over to her side, glancing at the workbook. "Let's see," I said, pointing at the equation. "Remember what Proverbs 2:6 says? 'For the Lord gives wisdom; from his mouth come knowledge and understanding.' You've got this."

Jessica nodded slowly, erasing her mistake and starting again with renewed focus.

Ethan finally stumbled into the kitchen, hair tousled and eyes barely open. "Mom, why do we have to get up so early?" he mumbled, slumping into his chair.

I smiled at him as I set a plate of pancakes in front of him. "Because early to bed and early to rise makes a man healthy, wealthy, and wise," I said, ruffling his hair. "Plus, it gives us time to read a Bible verse before school."

Jessica joined us at the table moments later, her sock triumphantly found and pulled onto her foot. She grabbed a piece of bacon and took a big bite. "What's today's verse?" she asked between chews.

I flipped open our well-worn family Bible to Psalm 119:105: "'Your word is a lamp for my feet, a light on my path.' Remember that as you go through your day," I told them.

The kids nodded as they finished their breakfast, their spirits lifted by the familiar routine. Despite the mayhem and noise that filled our mornings, there was an underlying sense of love woven through our routine—a love that thrived on Scripture and faith as much as it did on bacon and pancakes.

As I watched my children scarf down their breakfast, memories of my own childhood began to surface. I grew up in a home where faith was the cornerstone of our lives. My parents, both devout Christians, raised me with a firm but loving hand, instilling in me the same Biblical principles I now try to pass on to my own children.

My father was a man of few words but strong convictions. He believed that discipline was an essential part of raising a child in the fear and admonition of the Lord. My mother, on the other hand, had a gentler touch but was no less resolute when it came to matters of faith and obedience. They were a united front, and their rules were clear: respect God, respect others, and respect yourself.

One particular incident stands out vividly in my mind. I must have been about eight years old, and I had decided it would be a good idea to sneak a cookie from the jar before dinner. My mother had explicitly told me not to spoil my appetite, but the temptation proved too strong. I tiptoed into the kitchen, heart pounding with the thrill of rebellion, and reached into the jar.

Just as my fingers closed around the cookie, my father's voice boomed from behind me. "Sarah Ann! What are you doing?"

I froze, cookie in hand, my heart sinking. Turning slowly, I met his stern gaze. "I—I was just getting a cookie," I stammered, my voice barely above a whisper.

He didn't raise his voice or scold me harshly. Instead, he knelt down to look me in the eye. "Sarah," he said quietly, "what does Ephesians 6:1 say?"

"'Children, obey your parents in the Lord: for this is right,'" I recited reluctantly.

"That's right," he nodded. "And what did your mother tell you about cookies before dinner?"

"She said not to eat them," I admitted, feeling the weight of my disobedience.

He took the cookie from my hand and placed it back in the jar. "Obedience isn't just about following rules; it's about honoring your parents and ultimately honoring God." His words were firm but filled with love and conviction.

My mother appeared then, having heard everything from the doorway. She placed a gentle hand on my shoulder and guided me to sit at the kitchen table. "We discipline you because we love you," she said softly. "And because we want you to grow up knowing right from wrong."

That lesson stayed with me throughout my life—obedience rooted not in fear but in love and reverence for God's commandments. It's a lesson I hope to pass on to my own children through every breakfast conversation and bedtime prayer.

As I glanced at Jessica still munching on her bacon, Ethan now fully awake and chatting animatedly with Emily over math problems, I felt a swell of gratitude for the legacy of faith my parents had given me. It was a legacy I was determined to uphold in our own home, one Bible verse at a time.

I remember the evening John and I first discussed starting a family. We sat on the porch swing, the soft hum of crickets filling the air around us. The sun dipped below the horizon, casting a warm glow that seemed to wrap us in its embrace. John held my hand, his thumb gently tracing circles on my skin.

"Sarah," he began, his voice steady, "do you think we're ready for this? To bring children into this world?"

I looked into his eyes, seeing the same mix of excitement and apprehension that mirrored my own feelings. "I believe so, John. But it's not just about being ready. It's about being willing to raise them with the values we hold dear."

He nodded, a small smile playing at the corners of his lips. "I want our children to grow up knowing God, understanding His love and His commandments."

I squeezed his hand, feeling a surge of love and unity between us. "Just like our parents did for us," I agreed. "We need to give them a foundation that's unshakable, even if it means going against what society says is acceptable."

John's gaze grew more intense, his conviction clear. "It won't be easy," he admitted. "But I know we can do it together."

I took a deep breath, the weight of our decision settling over me like a comforting blanket. "We'll need to pray constantly for guidance and strength," I said softly. "And we must be prepared for the challenges that come with clinging to our values."

He nodded again, his grip on my hand tightening slightly as if to reassure both of us. "Our children will know right from wrong because we'll teach them from the Bible," he declared with unwavering resolve.

In that moment, sitting on our porch with the night slowly enveloping us, I felt an overwhelming sense of purpose. We weren't just planning to start a family; we were committing to raise souls in a way that honored God above all else.

"We'll face resistance," I mused aloud, thinking about how countercultural our approach might seem.

John leaned in closer, his voice almost a whisper but filled with strength. "We're not doing this for anyone else's approval," he reminded me. "We're doing this because it's what God calls us to do as parents."

I felt tears prick at the corners of my eyes, not from fear but from gratitude and determination. "Together then," I whispered back.

"Together," he affirmed.

In that sacred moment on our porch swing, under the watchful gaze of a thousand stars, John and I united in our shared vision for our future family—a vision built on faith, love, and unwavering commitment to raising our children in God's truth.

John and I sat on our porch swing, the soft hum of crickets filling the air around us. The sun dipped below the horizon, casting a warm glow that seemed to wrap us in its embrace. He held my hand, his thumb gently tracing circles on my skin.

"Sarah," he began, his voice steady, "do you think we're ready for this? To bring children into this world?"

I looked into his eyes, seeing the same mix of excitement and apprehension that mirrored my own feelings. "I believe so, John. But it's not just about being ready. It's about being willing to raise them with the values we hold dear."

He nodded, a small smile playing at the corners of his lips. "I want our children to grow up knowing God, understanding His love and His commandments."

I squeezed his hand, feeling a surge of love and unity between us.

I remember when John and I first started courting. It was a time when the world around us seemed to be moving in a different direction. Our peers often looked at us as though we were relics from another era. The idea of courtship, of saving intimacy for marriage, was almost laughable to many.

We had met at church, both of us deeply involved in various ministries. I admired his quiet strength and unwavering faith. One evening after Bible study, he approached me with a seriousness that took me by surprise.

"Sarah," he said, looking me directly in the eyes, "I'd like to court you with the intention of seeking God's will for our future together."

My heart fluttered, but I managed to keep my composure. "John, I would be honored."

From that moment, we embarked on a journey that was anything but conventional by modern standards. We set boundaries, choosing to avoid situations that might lead to temptation. It wasn't always easy; there were moments when the desire to break those boundaries was strong. But we prayed through those times, leaning on God's strength rather than our own.

Our courtship involved long conversations about our faith, our hopes for the future, and how we envisioned raising a family. We attended premarital counseling sessions at our church, seeking wisdom from older couples who had walked this path before us. They shared their experiences and offered invaluable advice that strengthened our resolve.

One afternoon after a particularly enlightening counseling session, John turned to me as we walked to the car.

"Sarah," he began, "I know this isn't the path most people choose today. But I'm grateful for it. I believe it's making us stronger."

I felt tears well up in my eyes as I nodded in agreement. "I feel the same way, John. This commitment to our beliefs is shaping us into who God wants us to be."

The months passed and our bond grew deeper. The commitment we had made—to honor God first and foremost—laid a foundation of trust and respect that carried us through even the most challenging times.

Reflecting on those days now, I see how countercultural our relationship truly was. But it was this very countercultural stance that fortified our marriage. It created a bond not easily shaken by the storms of life.

I remember the day Michael was born as if it were yesterday. The anticipation had been building for months, each day inching us closer to the moment we'd finally meet our son. When the contractions started, I felt a mixture of excitement and fear, emotions swirling together like a storm.

The drive to the hospital felt surreal. John held my hand, his grip firm but comforting. "We're almost there," he kept saying, though we both knew it wasn't about the destination but the journey we were about to embark on.

In the delivery room, time seemed to blur. The pain was intense, each contraction a reminder of the monumental task ahead. But amid the pain, there was also an overwhelming sense of purpose. I clung to my faith, praying silently for strength and guidance.

"You're doing great, Sarah," John encouraged, his voice steady despite the chaos around us.

Finally, after what felt like an eternity, Michael entered the world with a powerful cry. The nurses placed him on my chest, and in that instant, all the pain and exhaustion melted away. I looked down at his tiny face, marveling at the miracle of life. His eyes were closed tightly, his little fists clenched as if he were already preparing to take on the world.

Joy washed over me like a wave. "He's perfect," I whispered, tears streaming down my face.

John leaned in closer, his eyes filled with awe and gratitude. "Thank you, God," he murmured softly.

Holding Michael for the first time brought a profound sense of responsibility. The weight of motherhood settled on me like a mantle—a mantle I had longed for but now understood came with immense responsibility. I felt an overwhelming gratitude for this precious gift but also a deep-seated fear of not being enough for him.

As I lay there holding my newborn son, I made a silent vow. In that quiet moment amidst the bustling activity of doctors and nurses, I rededicated my life to raising Michael—and any children that followed—in God's way.

"Lord," I prayed silently, "give me the wisdom and strength to guide him according to Your will."

The emotions surged through me: joy at becoming a mother for the first time, awe at the miracle of life cradled in my arms, gratitude for this new chapter God had granted us. And yes, fear—fear of failing in this most sacred role. But even in that fear was a resolve strengthened by faith.

Michael's tiny fingers curled around mine as if he sensed my thoughts and offered his own kind of assurance. In that moment, I knew that by God's grace, I would strive every day to be the mother he deserved—one who would mold his soul according to His teachings.

And thus began our journey together—a journey marked by faith, love, and an unwavering commitment to raising our children in His ways.

The morning light filtered through the kitchen window, casting a warm glow over the cluttered table. Michael, Jessica, Ethan, and Emily sat together for breakfast, each immersed in their own morning rituals. Michael was flipping through his textbook, trying to cram in some last-minute studying. Jessica scrolled through her phone, occasionally rolling her eyes at something on the screen. Ethan was half-asleep, his head bobbing as he struggled to stay awake. And Emily, my sweet middle child, was scribbling furiously in her sketchbook between bites of cereal.

The table itself was a mess of dishes and food items—a half-empty carton of milk, a bowl of scrambled eggs, toast crumbs scattered everywhere. The sound of clinking spoons and muted conversation filled the room. It was chaotic, yet it felt right. It felt like home.

"Mom, can you help me with this math problem later?" Emily asked without looking up from her sketchbook.

"Of course," I replied, mentally making a note to carve out some time for her after school.

Suddenly, a loud clatter broke the peace as Ethan knocked over his glass of milk. The liquid spread quickly across the table, threatening to drench Jessica's phone and Michael's textbook.

"Ethan!" Jessica exclaimed, pulling her phone away just in time.

"Sorry!" Ethan scrambled to grab a napkin, his face flushed with embarrassment.

I moved quickly to help him clean up the mess. "It's okay, just be more careful next time," I said gently but firmly.

As I wiped up the spilled milk, I couldn't help but smile at the scene before me. This was family life—messy, imperfect, but full of love and grace. Each child had their quirks and challenges, but they were mine to nurture and guide.

In that moment, my inner resolve strengthened. My role as their mother wasn't just about keeping them fed and clothed; it was about shaping their hearts and minds according to God's will. I had to be both friend and disciplinarian, balancing love with firm boundaries.

I watched as Michael gave Ethan a reassuring pat on the back while Jessica teased him about his clumsiness. Emily remained absorbed in her art but glanced up occasionally with a knowing smile.

This daily chaos might have seemed overwhelming to some, but to me, it was a testament to our family's bond—a bond built on faith, love, and unwavering commitment. As I stood there amidst the cluttered dishes and spilled milk, I felt an overwhelming sense of purpose and gratitude.

"Alright everyone," I said brightly, "finish up your breakfast. We've got a busy day ahead."

Chapter 3

The Early Years

O ur home wasn't grand or extravagant, but it was alive with the hum of daily life. The walls were painted in warm, earthy tones, adorned with family photos and children's artwork. Each room held its own history, from the faded armchair in the living room that John refused to part with, to the kitchen table that bore the scars of countless family meals and craft projects.

The living room was the heart of our home, a cozy space filled with mismatched furniture that somehow fit together perfectly. Shelves crammed with books and board games lined one wall, while a piano stood proudly in the corner—an heirloom from my parents. The carpet was worn but clean, a testament to years of foot traffic and spontaneous dance parties.

In the midst of this warm chaos, I found myself chasing after young Michael. At three years old, he was a whirlwind of energy and curiosity. Today, he'd discovered the joy of pulling pots and pans out of the lower kitchen cabinets. The clanging sounds echoed through the house as he giggled uncontrollably.

"Michael! Come back here," I called out, trying to sound stern but failing miserably as I suppressed a laugh.

He darted around the kitchen island, his chubby legs moving faster than I thought possible. His laughter filled the room, infectious and pure. I couldn't help but smile as I watched him.

Just as he reached for another pot, I swooped in and scooped him up into my arms. "Gotcha!" I said triumphantly.

Michael squirmed playfully in my grasp, still laughing. "Mommy! Pots make music!"

I kissed his forehead and carried him over to the couch in the living room. "Yes, they do, but let's save your musical talents for later."

Settling onto the couch with Michael in my lap, I felt a deep sense of contentment wash over me. The house may have been in disarray, with toys strewn about and laundry waiting to be folded, but it was our haven—a place where love reigned supreme.

As Michael snuggled against me, his little hands clutching my shirt, I glanced around at our home. Despite its humble appearance and constant state of activity, it exuded warmth and joy. It was here that we lived out our faith daily, through shared meals, bedtime prayers, and moments like this—filled with laughter and love.

In that moment, amidst the cheerful chaos, I felt an overwhelming gratitude for our simple yet vibrant life.

I remember my pregnancy with Michael vividly, as if it were yesterday. The journey began with a wave of morning sickness that felt anything but mild. Every morning, like clockwork, I found myself hunched over the toilet, praying for relief. It was a humbling experience, one that made me appreciate the resilience of mothers everywhere.

Strange cravings soon followed, adding a peculiar twist to my daily routine. Pickles and ice cream became my go-to snack, much to John's amusement. He'd watch me with a bemused expression as I dipped the salty pickles into the creamy sweetness. "Are you sure that's good for the baby?" he'd tease, his eyes twinkling with love and concern.

Amidst the nausea and odd cravings, anxiety crept in like an uninvited guest. Would I be a good mother? Could I raise this child in the way of the Lord? The questions swirled in my mind, often keeping me up at night. I turned to prayer, seeking solace in the quiet moments before dawn. My faith was my anchor, steadying me through the waves of uncertainty.

As my belly grew rounder, so did my excitement. Each flutter and kick was a reminder of the life growing within me—a miraculous gift from God. John and I would spend evenings dreaming about our future as parents, our conversations filled with hope and anticipation.

In those months of waiting, my own mother became an invaluable source of wisdom and comfort. She had raised me with unwavering love and discipline, instilling in me the values that shaped my faith. Her presence was a balm to my anxious heart.

One afternoon, as we sat on the porch sipping lemonade, she shared stories of her own pregnancies—each one unique yet bound by the common thread of maternal love.

Her eyes sparkled with nostalgia as she recounted the challenges and joys she faced.

"Sarah," she said gently, placing her hand on mine, "motherhood is not about perfection. It's about grace—God's grace flowing through you to nurture and guide your child."

Her words resonated deeply within me. In that moment, I felt a profound connection to the generations of women who had come before me—mothers who had loved fiercely and prayed fervently for their children.

With each passing day, my excitement grew alongside my belly. I knew there would be challenges ahead, but I also knew that I was not alone. Surrounded by love and fortified by faith, I embraced the journey of motherhood with an open heart and unwavering trust in God's plan.

From the moment Michael was born, I knew that our home would be a place where faith was not just spoken about but lived out in every aspect. I wanted to instill in him a love for God's Word from the very beginning, even if he couldn't fully understand it yet.

Each night, as the house quieted down and the soft glow of the lamp filled his nursery, I would settle into the rocking chair with Michael cradled in my arms. His tiny eyes would flutter as I opened his first Bible—illustrated and full of colorful pictures designed to captivate a child's imagination. I read to him stories of Noah's ark, David and Goliath, and Daniel in the lion's den.

"God saved Noah and his family because they obeyed Him," I'd whisper softly, hoping the words would take root in his young heart.

Before laying him down in his crib, we would say a simple prayer together. "Dear Jesus," I'd begin, holding his little hands between mine, "thank you for today. Bless Mommy and Daddy. Help us to love you more each day. Amen." It was a small ritual, but it held profound significance. I believed that even if he couldn't yet grasp the meaning of those words, they were planting seeds that would one day bear fruit.

Mealtime was another opportunity to weave faith into our daily lives. As John and I gathered around the table with Michael in his high chair, we'd bow our heads and thank God for His provision.

"Dear Lord," John would say, his voice steady and sincere, "thank you for this food. Bless it to our bodies and help us to be grateful for your blessings. Amen."

Michael often babbled along with us, his chubby hands clapping with delight. It might have seemed like a small thing, but those moments were foundational in teaching him gratitude and reverence.

Our bedtime routine became a cherished time of connection and spiritual growth. After reading Bible stories, we'd sing hymns softly as he drifted off to sleep. "Jesus loves me, this I know," I'd sing gently, my voice blending with John's as we watched our son fall into slumber.

In those quiet moments, I felt a deep sense of purpose and fulfillment. I knew that these routines were more than just habits; they were the building blocks of Michael's spiritual foundation. Even if he couldn't understand everything now, I trusted that God was at work in his little heart, nurturing the seeds we diligently planted each day.

I still remember the first time I had to exercise real discipline on Michael. He was four years old, full of boundless energy and curiosity. We were in the kitchen; I was preparing dinner while he played with his toy cars on the floor. The scent of spaghetti sauce filled the room, and a hymn played softly in the background. It was a typical evening, or so I thought.

Out of nowhere, Michael decided he wanted a cookie before dinner. He toddled over to the pantry and started rummaging through it.

"Michael, no cookies before dinner," I said firmly, without raising my voice.

He ignored me, continuing his search. I walked over and gently closed the pantry door. "I said no, Michael."

His eyes flashed with defiance. "But I want one!" he shouted, his small fists clenching.

I knelt down to his level, trying to keep my voice calm. "We have to wait until after dinner, sweetie."

Without warning, he lashed out, smacking my arm with surprising force for someone so small. My heart sank. This wasn't just about a cookie anymore; it was about obedience and respect.

"Michael, we do not hit," I said sternly, taking his hand in mine.

His face contorted with anger as he yanked his hand away. "You're mean! I don't like you!" His words stung more than any physical blow could.

I stood there for a moment, grappling with how to respond. My instinct was to comfort him, but I knew that wouldn't address the issue at hand. I needed to be nurturing but also firm—a delicate balance that felt almost impossible in that moment.

Taking a deep breath, I looked him in the eye. "Michael, go to your room and think about what you did."

He stomped off, tears streaming down his face. As I watched him go, my own eyes filled with tears. It broke my heart to see him so upset, but I knew that teaching him right from wrong was an act of love.

I turned back to the stove, stirring the sauce absent-mindedly as I prayed silently for wisdom and strength. The weight of that moment pressed heavily on me; this was the first real test of my commitment to raising my children by biblical principles.

After a few minutes—though it felt like an eternity—I went to his room and found him sitting on his bed, still sniffling.

"Michael," I began softly but firmly...

I stood outside Michael's door, heart pounding. The decision weighed heavily on me. The Bible spoke of "the rod of correction" and the importance of discipline, but knowing it and doing it felt worlds apart.

I opened the door slowly and saw Michael's tear-streaked face. He looked up at me, eyes filled with both defiance and sorrow. My own eyes misted over, but I had to stay resolute.

"Michael," I began, my voice trembling slightly, "when you hit Mommy, you disobeyed. The Bible tells us that children must obey their parents in the Lord, for this is right."

His lower lip quivered. "I'm sorry, Mommy."

"I know you are," I said softly. "But there are still consequences for our actions." I took a deep breath. "Come here."

He hesitated but eventually walked over to me. I guided him gently to the bed and laid him across my lap. My hands shook as I raised them, but I remembered Proverbs 13:24—"Whoever spares the rod hates their children, but the one who loves their children is careful to discipline them." It wasn't about punishment; it was about teaching.

I administered the spanking—three firm swats—and each one felt like a dagger to my heart. Michael cried out with each one, his little body writhing in my lap. When it was over, I lifted him up and he clung to me immediately, sobbing into my shoulder.

I held him close, rubbing his back soothingly. "I love you so much, Michael," I whispered into his ear. "I discipline you because I love you and want you to grow up knowing right from wrong."

His sobs began to subside as he nestled into my embrace. "Do you really love me?" he asked between hiccups.

"More than anything in this world," I assured him, kissing the top of his head.

We stayed like that for several minutes—him clinging to me for comfort and me holding him with all the love a mother could muster. Eventually, he pulled back and looked at me with tear-filled eyes.

"I'm sorry," he whispered again.

"I forgive you," I replied softly. "But remember why we have rules—it's because we love each other and want what's best for each other."

He nodded solemnly, wiping his tears with the back of his hand. I stood up and held out my hand to him.

"Come on," I said with a gentle smile. "Let's go finish dinner together."

After our difficult moment, I needed a reprieve as much as Michael did. We made our way to the living room, where a pile of storybooks awaited us. He picked out his favorite, "The Little Engine That Could," and snuggled up next to me on the couch.

"Read this one, Mommy," he requested, his earlier tears forgotten.

"Of course, sweetheart," I replied, opening the well-worn pages. As I read about the brave little engine climbing the hill, Michael's eyes lit up with wonder. His tiny fingers traced the illustrations, and he giggled at the silly faces the characters made.

Finishing the story, I suggested, "How about we bake some cookies together?"

Michael's face brightened. "Yes! Can we make chocolate chip?"

"Absolutely," I said with a smile. We headed to the kitchen and gathered the ingredients. Michael stood on a stool beside me, his small hands eager to help mix the dough. Flour dusted his cheeks as he stirred vigorously, and I couldn't help but laugh.

"You've got flour everywhere!" I teased, wiping a smudge from his nose.

He giggled in response. "It's snowing in the kitchen!"

As we shaped the cookies together, Michael's laughter filled the room. His joy was contagious. These moments—these simple, joyful moments—made all the struggles of parenting worthwhile.

While waiting for the cookies to bake, we sat at the table with crayons and paper. Michael drew pictures of trains and animals while I sketched alongside him.

"Look, Mommy! It's you and me," he said proudly, holding up a drawing of two stick figures holding hands.

My heart swelled with love. "It's beautiful, Michael."

Though discipline was hard and often heart-wrenching, these were the moments I cherished—the bonding times that built our relationship. Through playtime and shared activities, I could see his heart softening and our connection growing stronger.

The timer dinged, signaling that our cookies were ready. Michael jumped off his chair with excitement as we pulled out the warm treats from the oven. We sat back down at the table with a plateful of cookies and two glasses of milk.

"These are delicious," Michael said through a mouthful of cookie.

I laughed. "I think you did most of the work."

He beamed with pride, crumbs clinging to his lips. As we enjoyed our treat together, I thanked God for these precious moments—moments that reminded me why discipline was necessary but love was essential.

When Jessica was born, our home transformed almost overnight. Michael, who had been the sole focus of our attention, now had a little sister to share the spotlight with. At first, he didn't quite understand why this tiny new person needed so much of my time.

"Why does she cry so much?" he asked one afternoon, standing beside the crib with a puzzled expression.

"She's just a baby, Michael," I explained gently. "Crying is how she tells us what she needs."

He seemed to accept that answer, at least for the moment. Watching him interact with Jessica brought me immense joy. He would bring her toys and mimic the way I talked to her, his voice soft and caring. It warmed my heart to see the budding bond between them.

As Jessica grew older and more mobile, new challenges emerged. There were times when Michael felt left out or jealous of the attention she received. Once, while I was nursing Jessica, Michael came up and tugged at my sleeve.

"Mommy, can you play trains with me?" he asked, his eyes filled with longing.

"In just a minute, sweetheart," I replied. "Let me finish feeding Jessica."

Michael sighed but waited patiently. Balancing time between them was an ongoing struggle, but I tried to involve him in caring for his sister whenever possible. We turned diaper changes into games and made bath time a family event.

The dynamic shifted again when Ethan arrived. With three children under one roof, our home buzzed with constant activity. Michael and Jessica now had another sibling to share their world with, and while it brought more chaos and noise, it also brought more love.

Jessica took to her role as an older sister with enthusiasm. She would mimic my actions, gently rocking Ethan in his bassinet or singing lullabies in her sweet toddler voice.

Yet there were moments when sibling rivalry reared its head.

One afternoon, I found Michael and Jessica arguing over a toy train set.

"That's mine!" Michael declared, clutching the engine tightly.

"No! Mine!" Jessica countered, tears welling up in her eyes.

Kneeling down between them, I tried to mediate. "How about we take turns? Sharing is important."

Reluctantly, they agreed. It wasn't always easy navigating their conflicts, but it taught them valuable lessons in patience and cooperation.

Despite the occasional squabbles, their bond grew stronger each day. Watching them play together in the backyard—Michael pushing Jessica on the swing while Ethan toddled around chasing butterflies—filled me with a sense of profound gratitude.

Our family might have been louder and messier than ever before, but it was also brimming with love and laughter. Each new addition brought unique challenges and immeasurable blessings. In those moments of togetherness, amidst the chaos and clamor, I saw God's grace at work in our home.

Reflecting on those early years, I felt a profound sense of peace wash over me. Sure, there were moments of chaos, sibling squabbles, and nights where sleep seemed like a distant dream. But amidst the challenges, a solid foundation was being laid.

I had always known that my role as a mother was not just to nurture but also to guide with unwavering standards. It wasn't about being popular or their friend. It was about something deeper, something eternal.

"Mom, why can't I go to the sleepover at Jenny's house?" Jessica had asked me one evening, her eyes pleading.

"Honey, we've talked about this," I replied, setting down my tea cup. "I don't know her parents well enough to be comfortable with you spending the night there."

She huffed and turned away, but deep down I knew this was what being a mother entailed—making tough decisions for their well-being.

Michael had his moments too. "Why do we have to read Bible stories every night?" he grumbled once, clearly preferring his comic books.

"Because," I answered calmly, "these stories teach us about God's love and how we should live our lives."

He rolled his eyes but didn't argue further. Over time, I noticed the lessons sinking in, even if they resisted initially. They began to understand that my firmness came from a place of love.

As they grew older and faced new challenges—peer pressure, school struggles, and the complexities of teenage life—I doubled down on my commitment. I wanted them to see that my love wasn't conditional on their happiness in the moment but rooted in their long-term spiritual well-being.

One evening after a particularly trying day, John sat beside me on the porch swing. "You're doing an incredible job," he said quietly.

I sighed deeply. "Sometimes it feels like they hate me."

"They don't," he reassured me. "They'll understand one day why you made the choices you did."

I leaned into him, grateful for his support. Together we had weathered many storms, and together we would continue to stand firm in our convictions.

Looking back now, I see those years as pivotal. They were the bedrock upon which our family's values were built. Yes, it cost me being their friend at times, but it solidified my role as their moral compass—a role I embraced wholeheartedly.

And in those quiet moments when they sought my guidance or came to me for comfort, I knew that our efforts were bearing fruit. The seeds we planted were growing into something beautiful and lasting.

Chapter 4

Turbulent Pre-Teens

A s my kids hit their pre-teen years, the household dynamic shifted like the tides. One minute, the house buzzed with laughter; the next, it simmered with tension.

"Mom, you don't understand anything!" Michael's voice echoed through the hallway as he slammed his bedroom door. He had entered that awkward phase where his voice cracked unpredictably, and his moods swung wildly.

I took a deep breath. "Michael, we need to talk about this calmly," I said through the closed door, my patience stretched thin.

The door stayed shut. Silence answered me.

Then there was Jessica, who seemed to change friend groups weekly. One day she loved reading and crafting; the next, she was all about sports and video games. Keeping up with her ever-evolving interests felt like running a marathon with no finish line in sight.

"Ethan, why do you always copy me?" Jessica snapped at her younger brother one afternoon. She had just come home from school and found him wearing a hat similar to hers.

Ethan looked down, fiddling with the brim of his hat. "I just thought it looked cool," he mumbled.

"Enough, both of you," I interjected, trying to keep my tone even. "Let's focus on being kind to each other."

Jessica rolled her eyes and muttered something under her breath as she stomped upstairs.

Even Ethan, usually my cheerful boy, had begun showing signs of resistance. Simple tasks like getting ready for school became battlegrounds.

"Ethan, you need to brush your teeth before bed," I reminded him one evening.

"Why do I have to do everything?" he groaned, dragging his feet towards the bathroom.

Through it all, I struggled to keep up with their rapid emotional and physical changes. One moment they craved independence; the next they needed reassurance. The whiplash left me feeling exhausted and uncertain.

At dinner one night, Jessica picked at her food silently while Michael argued with John about curfew times. Ethan sulked over not getting seconds on dessert.

I closed my eyes briefly, asking God for strength and wisdom. The challenges seemed unending and overwhelming at times, but I knew these moments were shaping them—and me—in ways only God understood.

Michael's defiance had become a storm cloud over our home. Each day brought new clashes and simmering tensions.

"Michael, it's time for youth group," I called from the kitchen, stirring a pot of spaghetti sauce.

He leaned against the doorway, arms crossed, eyes rolling. "Why do I have to go? It's so lame."

"It's important for you to be there," I said, trying to keep my voice steady. "You need the fellowship and teaching."

He scoffed, shaking his head. "I don't need a bunch of 'Jesus freaks' telling me how to live my life."

His words stung like nettles. I took a deep breath, gripping the wooden spoon tighter. "You do need it, Michael. And as long as you're under this roof, you will go."

His lips twisted into a sarcastic smirk. "Whatever you say, Bible-thumper."

I turned back to the stove, willing myself not to react. But inside, my heart ached at his mockery.

Later that evening, another battle erupted over video games. Michael had a penchant for pushing boundaries with the content he consumed.

"Michael, this game is rated M for mature," I said firmly, holding up the case he had left on the coffee table.

He shrugged, not looking up from his phone. "So what? It's just a game."

"It's not appropriate," I insisted. "You know our rules about what you're allowed to play."

"You're such a control freak," he muttered under his breath.

My patience wore thin. "Hand it over. Now."

He threw his phone onto the couch with exaggerated drama and snatched the game from my hand. "Fine! Here! Happy?"

"No, Michael," I replied quietly. "I'm not happy when you disobey and disrespect us."

As if that weren't enough for one night, we clashed again over his bedroom door policy.

"I need my privacy!" he argued when I told him to leave his door open while doing homework.

"And we need to ensure you're staying focused and safe," I countered.

"This is ridiculous!" He flung himself onto his bed, glaring at me from across the room.

"I'm your mother," I said softly but firmly. "And these rules are for your good."

"Yeah, yeah," he grumbled. "More 'Bible-thumper' rules."

I left his room feeling worn down by our constant conflicts. Michael's sarcastic refrains echoed in my mind long after I closed his door behind me.

As I walked back to the kitchen, I couldn't shake the unease gnawing at my heart. The world outside our home seemed determined to erode the values John and I had worked so hard to instill in our children. Pop culture had become a tidal wave of secular influences, sweeping over everything in its path.

The music blaring from Michael's room often set my teeth on edge. Lyrics glorifying rebellion, promiscuity, and materialism clashed violently with the biblical principles we taught at home. Every time I heard those beats thumping through the walls, I felt a knot tighten in my chest.

Television was no better. Shows that once seemed innocuous now teemed with messages that undermined our faith. Characters engaged in behaviors we found reprehensible, yet these were presented as normal, even desirable. The sitcoms laughed off promiscuity and mocked traditional family structures.

"Mom, everyone watches it," Jessica would argue when I expressed concern over a show she wanted to see. Her eyes would plead for leniency, but I stood firm.

Magazines lying around the house often made my stomach churn. Headlines screamed about celebrity scandals, fashion tips bordering on indecency, and lifestyles completely at odds with our beliefs.

Despite my best efforts to vet every piece of media that entered our home, I knew I couldn't control all their exposure. School was a battleground where peers brought their own influences. Michael came home humming tunes I'd never allow under our roof; Jessica talked about plotlines from shows she claimed "everyone" watched.

Even Ethan, my youngest, wasn't immune. He'd come back from playdates with new slang words that set off alarm bells in my head.

It felt like a losing battle sometimes. I'd sift through lyrics before allowing a new album, scrutinize movie ratings and reviews meticulously, even pre-read books for hidden agendas. But still, bits of the world's secular sediment seeped through.

"Mom," Michael once said when he caught me flipping through one of his magazines before handing it back to him. "You're being paranoid."

"I call it being protective," I replied, meeting his eyes with unwavering resolve.

But inside, doubt gnawed at me. How could I shield them from a culture that seeped into every corner of their lives? Each day brought new challenges and new influences vying for their attention.

I prayed constantly for wisdom and strength to guide them through this maze of modern temptations. The world may have its sway, but under our roof, I aimed to hold fast to the Rock of our faith.

Despite my worries and the endless vetting process, I knew one thing: God's grace would be our anchor amidst this storm of secularism.

Jessica stood in front of the mirror, adjusting the crop top that barely reached her midriff. I watched from the doorway, my heart sinking.

"Jessica, you can't wear that," I said, stepping into her room.

She turned to face me, eyes already brimming with defiance. "Why not? Everyone else does."

"Because it's immodest. It doesn't reflect the values we uphold in this house," I replied, trying to keep my voice steady.

Jessica rolled her eyes and turned back to the mirror. "You're such a prude, Mom."

The words stung, but I pressed on. "You know our rules about clothing. Crop tops, short shorts, low necklines—none of that leaves this house."

She spun around, tears now pooling in her eyes. "It's just clothes! Why do you have to make such a big deal out of everything?"

"Because it's not just about clothes," I said, my voice rising despite myself. "It's about respect—for yourself and for God."

Jessica's face crumpled. "Respect? How is wearing a crop top disrespectful?"

"It's about modesty and dignity," I explained, feeling the familiar knot tighten in my stomach. "Our bodies are temples of the Holy Spirit. We should honor them."

She crossed her arms over her chest, glaring at me through tear-filled eyes. "I feel like you're trying to control every aspect of my life."

"I'm not trying to control you; I'm trying to guide you," I said, taking a step closer.

"Well, it feels like control," she shot back, wiping angrily at her tears. "I just want to be like everyone else."

"And what if being like everyone else means compromising your values?" I asked softly.

Jessica looked away, the tension between us palpable. "I don't know," she whispered.

I took a deep breath, struggling to find the right words. "Look, I know it's hard to stand out and be different. But sometimes following God's path means going against what everyone else is doing."

She shook her head, tears streaming down her face now. "I hate this. I hate feeling like an outsider because of these stupid rules."

My heart ached seeing her so distressed. But I knew I couldn't relent on this. "I'm sorry you feel that way," I said quietly. "But these rules are here for a reason."

Jessica let out a frustrated scream and stormed past me out of the room.

As I watched her go, I prayed silently for strength and wisdom to navigate these turbulent teenage years without losing sight of our spiritual compass.

I sighed, running a hand through my hair as I watched Jessica storm off. Just then, Ethan wandered into the room, clutching his favorite stuffed bear. His eyes, wide and curious, reminded me of a time when life seemed simpler.

"Mom," he began tentatively, "can I watch that new show Michael talks about? The one with the superheroes?"

I knelt down to his level, feeling the familiar pang of concern. "Which show are you talking about, sweetheart?"

Ethan shuffled his feet. "The one with all the cool fights and explosions. Michael says it's awesome."

I knew immediately which show he meant. I'd already caught snippets of it and found it far too violent and graphic for his young mind. "Ethan, that show isn't appropriate for you. It's got too much fighting and bad language."

His face fell. "But Michael watches it all the time! And Jessica says it's not a big deal."

I felt my heart sink a little more. Michael's and Jessica's defiance had started to seep into Ethan's innocent world. "Just because your brother and sister watch something doesn't mean it's right for you," I explained gently.

Ethan frowned, his small brows knitting together in confusion. "But why not? It's just TV."

"It's more than just TV," I said softly, pulling him closer. "What we watch can affect how we think and feel. We need to fill our minds with good things, not violence or bad words."

He looked down at his bear, clearly wrestling with the idea. "So... no superheroes?"

"Not that kind of superhero," I replied with a small smile. "There are plenty of other shows you can enjoy that are good for you."

Ethan sighed deeply, mirroring a gesture I'd seen from his older siblings far too often lately. "Okay, Mom," he mumbled reluctantly.

As he turned to leave, I felt a wave of worry wash over me. The lines were blurring for him because of what Michael and Jessica had normalized in our home. It was a slippery slope—one where innocent inquiries could quickly turn into harmful habits.

"Ethan," I called after him.

He stopped and turned back to me, eyes still full of questions.

"I know it's hard when everyone else seems to be doing something different," I said, standing up and walking over to him. "But it's important to make choices that honor God."

He nodded slowly but didn't seem entirely convinced as he walked away.

I stood there in the silence of Jessica's room, praying for wisdom to navigate this maze of influences and hoping against hope that the seeds we planted would eventually bear fruit in all three of my children's lives.

That evening, as the kids retreated to their rooms, I found myself in the kitchen, leaning against the counter. John walked in, his face lined with concern but his eyes steady. He set his briefcase down and walked over to me.

"How was today?" he asked, his voice calm and reassuring.

"Another battle," I replied, feeling the weight of it all pressing down on my shoulders. "Jessica's still upset about the clothes, and Michael... well, you know how he is."

John nodded, stepping closer and placing a hand on my shoulder. "They'll understand one day. We're doing what's right."

I sighed deeply, grateful for his unwavering support. "Sometimes it feels like we're fighting a losing battle."

John smiled gently. "We're not fighting alone." He took my hand and led me to the living room. We knelt together by the couch, a familiar ritual that had seen us through many storms.

"Lord," John began, his voice steady and full of conviction, "give us strength to uphold Your principles in our home. Help us guide our children with wisdom and love."

As he prayed, I felt a sense of peace wash over me, a reminder that we were not carrying this burden by ourselves. "Father," I added when it was my turn, "soften our children's hearts to Your teachings. Help them see the love behind our rules."

We continued praying, lifting each child by name—Michael with his rebellious spirit, Jessica with her struggle for identity, and Ethan with his innocent questions. In those moments of shared faith and vulnerability, I felt our unity solidify even more.

John squeezed my hand as we finished. "We're in this together," he said firmly.

"Yes," I replied, feeling renewed determination. "Together."

We stood up slowly, lingering in the warmth of our shared resolve. John wrapped an arm around my shoulders as we walked back to the kitchen.

"They'll thank us one day," he murmured.

"I hope so," I said softly.

"We just have to stay strong," John continued. "The world may change its standards, but ours come from a higher place."

I nodded, feeling a fresh wave of strength and commitment rise within me. We were a team—unified in purpose and grounded in faith—ready to face whatever challenges came our way together.

One Sunday after service, I found myself lingering in the fellowship hall, scanning the room for a familiar face. I spotted Mrs. Thompson, the pastor's wife, chatting with a group of women. Taking a deep breath, I walked over.

"Sarah!" she greeted warmly, her eyes kind and knowing. "How are you?"

I tried to muster a smile but felt my composure cracking. "Could we talk for a moment?" My voice wavered.

She nodded, understanding immediately. "Of course, let's find somewhere quiet."

We settled in one of the church's small meeting rooms, and as soon as the door closed behind us, the tears came. Mrs. Thompson handed me a tissue and waited patiently as I struggled to gather myself.

"It's just been so hard," I confessed through sobs. "Michael's rebelliousness, Jessica's insistence on immodest clothes... I feel like I'm failing them."

Mrs. Thompson placed a comforting hand on mine. "Sarah, every parent goes through challenging seasons with their children. You're not alone."

I looked up at her, seeking solace in her experienced eyes. "How did you manage?"

She smiled softly. "Perseverance and prayer. There were times I cried out to God, wondering if we were making any difference at all. But remember, these struggles are phases—they will pass."

I nodded slowly, trying to absorb her words.

"Lean into your faith," she continued. "God sees your efforts and hears your prayers. You're planting seeds that will bear fruit in His time."

Her words brought a measure of peace, but my heart still felt heavy. "I just want to do right by them."

"And you are," she reassured me gently. "Trust that God will honor your faithfulness."

Later that week, I found myself sitting across from Mrs. Peters during our women's Bible study. She was an older mom whose children had all grown up and left home.

"I heard you've been having a tough time," she said kindly after the study ended.

I sighed deeply. "It feels like everything we're doing is being met with resistance."

Mrs. Peters nodded sympathetically. "I've been there too," she said softly. "It can be incredibly disheartening."

I looked at her hopefully.

"The key is perseverance," she continued firmly. "Keep standing firm on biblical principles and keep praying for your children. God's word does not return void."

Tears welled up again as I listened to her wisdom.

"Sarah," she added, leaning forward slightly, "lean into your faith during these tough times. The Lord will see you through."

One evening, after a particularly trying day, I found myself sitting at the kitchen table, staring blankly at the cluttered remains of dinner. Michael had stormed off to his room after another argument about his video games, Jessica had given me the silent treatment over her choice of clothing, and even little Ethan had thrown a tantrum over being denied a TV show. My heart felt like it was carrying the weight of the world.

I dropped my head into my hands, tears slipping through my fingers. "Lord," I whispered, "am I doing this all wrong?" The question hung in the air, heavy and raw. My resolve seemed to waver in the face of relentless defiance and the emotional toll it took on me.

John entered the kitchen quietly, placing a gentle hand on my shoulder. "Sarah," he said softly, "it's going to be okay."

I looked up at him, eyes red and swollen. "Is it? Every day feels like a battle. I just don't know if I can keep this up."

He pulled up a chair and sat beside me. "We knew this wouldn't be easy. But remember why we're doing this."

I wiped my tears with the back of my hand. "It just feels like we're losing them," I admitted.

John took my hand in his. "We're not losing them, Sarah. We're guiding them through rough waters. It's hard now, but we're building something lasting."

I wanted to believe him. Deep down, I knew he was right. But the daily struggle felt overwhelming. "I just want them to understand it's because we love them."

"They will," John assured me. "In time, they will."

I sighed deeply, feeling both exhausted and somewhat reassured by his presence. As we sat there in silence, an inner strength began to stir within me again.

"You're right," I finally said, squeezing his hand. "We can't give up now. They need us to stand firm."

John nodded in agreement. "We'll get through this together."

I stood up and began clearing the table with renewed determination. Yes, it was hard—sometimes unbearably so—but giving in wasn't an option. Popularity might be a casualty in this battle for their souls, but maintaining our standards was non-negotiable.

As I finished tidying up and prepared for bed that night, I prayed for strength and wisdom to keep fighting the good fight. Despite the challenges ahead, my commitment remained unwavering: raising our children according to God's principles was worth every tear and struggle.

The road was long and often lonely, but by God's grace, it was a path I would continue to walk steadfast

Chapter 5

Teenage Rebellion

I remember the shift like it happened yesterday. The boys, once inseparable in their shared adventures and secret handshakes, had grown apart. The rift widened with each passing day, Michael's teenage cynicism and rebellion driving a wedge between them.

Michael lounged on the couch one evening, his eyes glued to a screen that blared aggressive music videos. Ethan, who used to sit beside him and share in the excitement of whatever new interest Michael had, now stood awkwardly at the doorway. His eyes flickered with a mixture of hope and dread.

"Can I watch too?" Ethan asked, his voice timid.

Michael didn't even glance up. "This isn't for babies," he muttered.

Ethan's face fell, the sting of his brother's words clear. "I'm not a baby," he protested, though it lacked conviction.

Michael finally looked at him, his eyes filled with teenage disdain. "Then stop acting like one."

Ethan clenched his fists, frustration bubbling just beneath the surface. He turned away, muttering something under his breath as he retreated to his room.

I watched from the kitchen, my heart aching at the scene unfolding before me. This wasn't how it used to be. They used to be best buddies—partners in every escapade and defenders of each other against the world. Now, Michael's harshness seemed relentless, and Ethan's resentment was palpable.

Later that night, I found Ethan sitting on his bed, staring at a photo of him and Michael from happier times—both grinning widely at some forgotten joke.

"Hey there," I said softly as I entered his room.

He looked up, trying to hide the tears welling in his eyes. "Why does he hate me now?"

I sat beside him, pulling him into a comforting hug. "He doesn't hate you, Ethan. He's going through a lot of changes and sometimes that makes people act out."

"But why take it out on me?" His voice cracked with hurt.

"Because you're here," I explained gently. "You're safe for him to vent his frustrations on because deep down, he knows you love him no matter what."

Ethan shook his head. "It doesn't feel like love."

"I know it's hard," I admitted, my own heart breaking for him. "But this is just a phase. It won't last forever."

Ethan didn't seem convinced, but he nodded anyway, snuggling closer for comfort.

As I held him close, I prayed silently for wisdom and patience—for both my boys to find their way back to each other amidst the chaos of these turbulent years.

Jessica had always been my strong-willed child. From the moment she could talk, she had opinions and wasn't afraid to voice them. But as she entered high school, something changed. Her once bright and bubbly demeanor grew sullen, and her clothing choices shifted from modest dresses to ripped jeans and revealing tops.

One evening, I heard a commotion in the hallway. Jessica's voice rose in anger, laced with language I never thought I'd hear from her lips. "You don't understand me!" she screamed at John.

"Jess," I called out, stepping into the fray, "what's going on?"

She glared at me with a defiance that cut deep. "Why do you care? You just want to control me!"

My heart ached at her words, but I remained calm. "We care because we love you."

"Love?" she scoffed, rolling her eyes. "You mean rules and restrictions."

The tension between us escalated daily. She'd come home smelling of smoke, her eyes red and glassy. I tried to approach her gently one night after catching a whiff of cigarette smoke on her clothes.

"Jessica," I began, keeping my voice steady, "were you smoking?"

She crossed her arms defensively. "So what if I was? It's not like you can stop me."

Her dismissive attitude pierced through my resolve. "It's not about stopping you; it's about caring for your health."

"Whatever," she muttered before storming off to her room.

The final straw came one night when I heard the creak of our front door around midnight. My heart pounded as I crept down the stairs and found Jessica sneaking out.

"Where do you think you're going?" My voice trembled with a mix of anger and fear.

She froze, caught in the act. "Out," she replied defiantly.

"It's past curfew," I reminded her, struggling to keep my emotions in check.

"Curfew?" She laughed bitterly. "I'm not a child anymore."

I took a deep breath, praying for strength. "You're still under our roof, and there are rules."

"Rules," she repeated mockingly. "I'm done with your rules."

Before I could respond, she turned and ran out into the night

It was as if Jessica had found the embodiment of every worldly influence we'd tried to shield her from in one person. His name was Tyler. He was older, tattooed, and had a reputation that sent shivers down my spine. The first time he showed up at our doorstep, I knew trouble had found its way into our home.

Jessica introduced him with a defiant gleam in her eye. "This is Tyler," she said, almost daring me to react.

"Nice to meet you," I managed to say, extending my hand.

He smirked and shook it briefly, his grip too firm. "Likewise."

The nights Jessica spent out grew longer, and her defiance sharper. One evening, after she missed dinner again, I decided it was time to set boundaries.

"Jessica," I called as she walked through the door well past curfew. "We need to talk."

"About what?" she snapped, throwing her bag on the floor.

"About Tyler and your behavior lately," I replied, struggling to keep my voice steady.

Her eyes flashed with anger. "What about it? He's my boyfriend, and you can't control who I date."

"It's not about control," I insisted. "It's about your well-being."

"You don't know him!" she yelled, her voice echoing through the house.

"I know enough," I said firmly. "And I'm worried."

"Worried? Or just trying to control my life?" She crossed her arms and glared at me.

My patience frayed. "Jessica, he's not good for you. Look at the choices you're making since you started seeing him!"

Her face twisted in rage. "You don't understand anything! You're stuck in your Bible-thumping world while I'm trying to live my life!"

"Living your life shouldn't mean compromising your values!" My voice rose despite my efforts to stay calm.

"My values? Or yours?" she shot back. "I'm sick of living under your rules!"

The screaming matches became routine. Each confrontation seemed to push her further away. Tyler's presence only fueled her rebellion. She'd come home with stories of parties and friends that made my heart ache with worry.

One night, after another explosive argument, Jessica stormed out of the house again. I sank onto the couch, tears streaming down my face. John came over and wrapped his arms around me.

"We're losing her," I whispered between sobs.

"We have to keep praying," he said softly, his voice steady even as mine broke.

Michael's rebellion took a different turn. Unlike Jessica's outward defiance, his battles were fought behind closed doors. He began isolating himself, locking himself in his room for hours. The change was abrupt, leaving me unsettled and worried.

One evening, I walked past his room and caught a whiff of something unmistakable—marijuana. My heart sank. I knocked on his door, hoping against hope that I was wrong.

"Michael, can we talk?"

No response.

I knocked again, louder this time. "Michael!"

Finally, the door creaked open. His eyes met mine, glazed and distant. The smell hit me stronger now, confirming my worst fears.

"What's going on in here?" I asked, trying to keep my voice steady.

"Nothing," he mumbled, looking past me as if I weren't there.

"Michael," I said more firmly, "this is not nothing. Your room reeks of marijuana."

"So what?" His voice was flat, devoid of the fire that usually accompanied our arguments.

I stepped into the room, my eyes scanning for any signs of harder drugs or alcohol. My heart pounded as I opened

drawers and lifted up his mattress, desperate to find something—anything—that would give me a clue to the depth
of his self-destruction.

"Mom, stop it," he said weakly, but made no move to stop
me.

I found nothing concrete but that did little to ease my
mind. The fear gnawed at me—was there more hidden
somewhere else? Was he doing harder drugs? Self-harm-
ing?

I turned to him. "Michael, please talk to me. What's going
on with you?"

He shrugged, his eyes dull and lifeless. "Nothing you can
fix."

His words cut deep. "I'm your mother," I insisted. "I need
to know if you're okay."

He looked away, a tear escaping down his cheek. "Just
leave me alone."

That night, after everyone else had gone to bed, I sat in
the living room with my Bible open but unread in my lap.
The weight of worry pressed down on me like a physical
burden.

John joined me after a while. "Any luck?" he asked softly.

I shook my head. "He's shutting us out completely."

"We have to keep trying," John said resolutely.

"I know," I replied through tears. "But it's tearing us
apart."

Thanksgiving had always been a cherished tradition in
our family, a day when we gathered with extended relatives
to give thanks and enjoy a feast. But this year, the tension
was palpable from the moment we walked into my sister's

home. The kids were on edge, and I could feel the weight of our unresolved conflicts pressing down on me.

As we settled around the long dining table, I caught Michael and Jessica exchanging a look that made my stomach churn. Something was brewing, and I feared it would boil over before the day was done.

Dinner started smoothly enough. The usual clatter of plates and cheerful chatter filled the room. But as soon as grace was said, Michael leaned back in his chair, crossing his arms defiantly.

"So, Mom," he began loudly, drawing everyone's attention. "Are you gonna tell everyone here about your latest ban? Or should I?"

I felt my cheeks flush. "Michael, this isn't the time."

"Oh, come on," he continued, ignoring my plea. "Aunt Linda might like to know why you won't let us watch anything that's not 'Christian-approved.'"

The room fell silent. All eyes turned to me, waiting for my response. My heart pounded in my chest as I tried to maintain my composure.

"We have rules in our house for a reason," I said firmly.

"Rules that are ridiculous!" Jessica chimed in, slamming her fork down on her plate. "You treat us like prisoners."

I glanced at John for support, but his eyes were fixed on his plate, avoiding the confrontation.

"Jessica," I began softly but firmly, "we've talked about this—"

"No!" she interrupted, her voice rising. "I'm tired of talking! You're ruining our lives with your outdated rules!"

The room felt like it was closing in on me. Relatives shifted uncomfortably in their seats, trying to pretend they weren't listening to our family drama unfold.

"Enough," I said, standing up and raising my voice to be heard over the rising tide of rebellion. "This is not the time or place for this discussion."

Michael stood up as well, his face red with anger. "Why not? You never listen at home anyway! Maybe here you'll finally get it."

I took a deep breath, feeling every eye in the room on me. This was a moment that demanded strength and resolve.

"I am your mother," I said slowly and deliberately. "And as long as you live under our roof, you will follow our rules."

After Thanksgiving, the atmosphere at home grew increasingly strained. It wasn't just the kids who were fracturing; John and I started clashing in ways we never had before. I felt like a storm cloud constantly hanging over our house, and John seemed to be drifting further away each day.

One evening, after yet another heated argument with Michael, I found John waiting for me in the kitchen. He leaned against the counter, arms crossed, a look of frustration etched on his face.

"Sarah, we need to talk," he began, his voice low but firm.

I sighed, rubbing my temples. "What now, John?"

"You're too harsh on them," he said bluntly. "Especially Michael. He's not a child anymore; he's almost an adult."

"And that's precisely why we need to be firm!" I shot back, my voice rising. "If we let up now, what kind of adults will they become?"

John shook his head. "There's a difference between being firm and being unreasonable. You're pushing them away."

"Unreasonable?" I echoed, feeling my blood boil. "I'm trying to save them from making terrible mistakes! You saw how Michael acted at Thanksgiving. If we don't set boundaries—"

"We are setting boundaries," John interrupted, his eyes narrowing. "But there's no grace in how you're enforcing them. You're not listening to them."

"And you're too permissive!" I countered. "You let them walk all over you! They need discipline, not leniency."

John's jaw tightened. "It's not about leniency. It's about understanding where they're coming from. They're growing up in a different world than we did."

I turned away from him, trying to control my emotions. The tension between us felt like a chasm that was growing wider by the day.

"You think I don't know that?" I whispered, tears welling up in my eyes despite my best efforts to hold them back.

John softened slightly but remained resolute. "I just think we need to find a balance, Sarah."

"Balance," I muttered under my breath as if the word itself was foreign and unachievable in our current state.

We stood there in silence for a moment, the weight of our differing views pressing down on us like an invisible burden.

"We both want what's best for them," John finally said softly.

I nodded reluctantly. "But we can't seem to agree on what that is."

The night everything fell apart, I was jolted awake by the phone ringing. Groggy and disoriented, I glanced at the clock. It was 2:17 AM. John stirred beside me, mumbling something incoherent.

"Hello?" I answered, my voice thick with sleep.

"Mrs. Blake?" a stern voice on the other end asked. "This is Officer Thompson from the County Sheriff's Department. We have your son, Michael, in custody."

My heart sank. "What happened?"

"He was involved in a car accident," the officer explained. "We suspect he was under the influence of marijuana."

I felt like the ground had dropped out from under me. "Is he...is he okay?"

"He's not injured, but he's facing serious charges," Officer Thompson replied.

By the time John and I reached the police station, my mind was racing with a thousand thoughts. How had it come to this? We had tried so hard to instill biblical values and moral discipline in our children, but now our eldest son was sitting in a jail cell.

Michael looked up as we walked in, his eyes red and filled with regret. He seemed so small, so vulnerable behind those bars.

"Mom, Dad..." His voice cracked.

"Michael," I managed to say, fighting back tears.

John stepped forward, his face a mix of anger and concern. "What were you thinking?"

Michael's shoulders slumped. "I don't know. I wasn't thinking."

"We're here now," I said softly, though my heart felt like it was shattering into pieces.

After signing some paperwork and talking with the officer about what would come next legally, we finally got Michael released on bail. The ride home was silent, tension hanging thick in the air.

Back at home, we gathered in the living room. The dim light cast long shadows on our faces.

"I just...I just wanted to fit in," Michael finally admitted, tears streaming down his face. "I'm sorry."

His words cut deep. All those years of trying to be both a mother and a moral guide seemed to unravel before my eyes.

"Fitting in doesn't mean throwing away everything we've taught you," John said firmly but gently.

"I know," Michael whispered, looking down at his hands.

I took a deep breath, trying to steady myself. "This is a wake-up call for all of us."

I found myself on my knees more often than ever before. The living room floor became my sanctuary, the place where I cried out to God with all the fervor of a mother on the brink of despair. Every creak of the house, every rustle of the leaves outside, seemed to echo the turmoil within my heart.

"Lord, I don't know what to do," I whispered one night, my voice barely audible over the sound of my own sobbing. "I thought I was raising them right. Where did I go wrong?"

The Scriptures became my lifeline. Isaiah 40:31 - "But they who wait for the Lord shall renew their strength; they shall mount up with wings like eagles; they shall run and not be weary; they shall walk and not faint." I clung to those words as if they were a buoy in a stormy sea.

Each Sunday, I found solace in our church community. Pastor Thompson's sermons felt like direct messages from God, each word a balm to my wounded spirit. And the women—those steadfast, godly women—surrounded me with prayers and encouragement. Ruth, an elder's wife, would often sit with me after service, her hand gently squeezing mine.

"Sarah," she would say, her voice filled with unwavering conviction, "God is not done with your children yet. Keep praying."

And pray I did. My prayers turned raw and unfiltered. One night, alone in my room, I poured out my heart like never before.

"Father," I began, my voice cracking under the weight of my sorrow. "I come to You broken and desperate. My children...my precious Michael and Jessica...they're lost in this world. I've tried so hard to guide them Your way, but I've failed."

Tears streamed down my face as I continued, "Please, Lord, bring them back to You. Break the chains that bind them to these worldly influences. Let Your love flood their hearts and wash away their rebellion."

My hands clenched into fists as I pleaded, "Help me to be strong for them. Give me wisdom beyond my understanding. And Father, if it is Your will...please return my prodigals home."

I stayed there for what felt like hours, letting every tear and every word be a testament of my unwavering faith amidst the storm.

In those moments of fervent prayer, surrounded by Scripture and strengthened by the mentors at church, I found a glimmer of hope—a divine assurance that God was still at work in our lives.

One late afternoon, as the sun dipped low and painted the sky with hues of orange and pink, I found myself alone in the kitchen, scrubbing dishes with a vigor that matched my restless heart. The house was unusually quiet. John was still at work, and the kids were scattered in their rooms, each absorbed in their own worlds.

The phone rang, shattering the stillness. I dried my hands hastily and picked it up.

"Mom," Michael's voice came through the line, hesitant and fragile.

"Michael?" I felt a mix of relief and anxiety. "Is everything alright?"

"I... I need to talk to you."

"Of course, son. What's going on?"

There was a pause on the other end, filled only by his uneven breathing. Then, he began to speak in a rush, words tumbling over each other.

"I went to this thing... a meeting on campus. A guy from one of my classes invited me. It was like a Bible study, but different. People were sharing their stories, talking about struggles and faith."

My heart quickened as he continued.

"And Mom, I... I felt something. Something I haven't felt in a long time. It was like... like God was there with me. Like He hadn't given up on me."

Tears welled up in my eyes as I listened to my son's confession.

"Michael," I managed to say, my voice trembling with emotion. "God has never given up on you. And neither have I."

He took a deep breath before continuing. "I know I've messed up a lot. I've said things, done things I'm not proud of. But tonight... tonight felt different. I felt like there was hope for me again."

A glimmer of light pierced through the darkness that had surrounded us for so long. My heart swelled with gratitude and hope.

"Michael," I said softly, "this is just the beginning. God has plans for you, plans to prosper you and not to harm you."

"I want to come home this weekend," he said, his voice steadying with newfound resolve.

"We'd love that," I replied, tears streaming down my face unchecked now.

As we hung up the phone, I stood there for a moment, overwhelmed by the magnitude of what had just happened. One of my prodigals was finding his way back to truth.

It wasn't the end of our struggles; far from it. But it was a beacon of hope—a reminder that God was still working in our lives, guiding us back to Him one step at a time.

Chapter 6

Seeing the Fruits

T he house felt unbearably silent that evening, the kind of quiet that presses down on your soul. I knelt by my bedside, hands clasped together, tears streaming down my face.

"Lord," I whispered, voice breaking. "I don't know what else to do. Please, bring my child back to You. Show them Your love and grace."

The words tumbled out between sobs, a mother's desperate plea. I poured out my heart, every ounce of pain and hope mingling in the quiet of that room.

"Father, I've tried so hard to raise them in Your ways. But I can't reach them anymore. Only You can touch their hearts now. Please, Lord... please."

As the last words left my lips, a profound silence settled over me. It was as if time itself held its breath. I remained there, kneeling in prayer, eyes closed, seeking some sign of divine intervention.

Then, a soft knock echoed through the stillness.

I wiped my eyes hastily and rose to answer the door. My heart pounded in my chest as I turned the knob.

Standing there was Michael. His eyes were red-rimmed and filled with tears. He looked at me with an expression I hadn't seen in years—one of vulnerability and remorse.

"Mom," he said softly, his voice trembling. "Can we talk?"

My heart leapt within me as I stepped aside to let him in. He walked in slowly, almost as if he were afraid he'd be turned away.

We sat on the edge of my bed, the room filled with an unspoken understanding. He took a deep breath before speaking.

"I've made so many mistakes," he began, voice choked with emotion. "I thought I could handle everything on my own, but... I was wrong."

I placed a hand on his shoulder, feeling the tension and pain radiating from him.

"I'm so sorry," he continued, tears spilling down his cheeks. "For everything I've done and said."

In that moment, all the prayers and heartache seemed worth it. Here was my son—broken but reaching out for healing.

"Michael," I said gently, "you are always welcome here. No matter what you've done or where you've been, you're still my child."

He looked at me then with such raw honesty that it took my breath away.

"I want to come back," he whispered. "Not just home... but back to God."

We embraced then, both of us weeping—tears of sorrow mingled with joy.

God had answered my prayer in ways I could never have imagined.

We sat on the edge of my bed, and I watched as Michael struggled to find the words. His hands fidgeted in his lap, fingers twisting together like tangled threads.

"Mom," he began, voice barely above a whisper. "I've... I've done things I'm not proud of."

He took a deep breath, eyes avoiding mine. "I started smoking weed to fit in with my friends. At first, it was just to escape... everything. But it got worse. I started drinking too, and there were nights I don't even remember."

My heart clenched as he spoke, each word a knife to my soul.

"And it's not just that," he continued, tears now streaming freely down his face. "I lied to you and Dad. So many times. About where I was going, who I was with... I even stole money from you guys to buy more drugs."

I felt the sting of betrayal but forced myself to listen without judgment.

"I thought the world had more to offer," he admitted, voice breaking. "Parties, friends who seemed so cool, music that filled the emptiness for a while. But it never lasted. It was all so hollow."

He paused, wiping his face with the back of his hand.

"I got involved with some bad people," he confessed, eyes now meeting mine with a raw honesty that pierced through the hurt. "People who led me down darker paths than I ever thought I'd go."

The room seemed to close in around us as he laid bare the depth of his rebellion.

"I felt so lost," he said quietly. "Like I'd gone too far to ever come back."

He looked away again, shame evident in every line of his face.

"But then... something happened," he continued after a long pause. "I hit rock bottom. One night, after a particularly bad trip, I found myself alone and scared out of my mind."

He looked back at me then, eyes pleading for understanding.

"I remembered what you used to tell me," he said softly. "That no matter how far we stray, God is always waiting for us with open arms."

His voice broke completely then.

"I prayed that night," he whispered through his tears. "For the first time in years, I prayed. And... something changed inside me."

Michael took another deep breath, steeling himself for what came next.

"I re-accepted Christ into my heart," he said firmly but emotionally drained. "I begged Him for forgiveness and promised to turn my life around."

He looked at me with such raw vulnerability that it brought fresh tears to my eyes.

"Mom," he said, voice cracking again. "Can you forgive me? For all of it?"

"Of course, Michael," I said, voice trembling with emotion. "I forgive you. I always have."

We hugged tightly, the weight of years of pain and rebellion melting away in that single embrace. It felt like the first step toward mending what had been broken.

In the days that followed, Michael and I began to rebuild our relationship, piece by piece. Each morning, we shared breakfast together—just simple meals of scrambled eggs or pancakes—but they became sacred times of connection.

"Mom, can you pass the syrup?" Michael asked one morning, a soft smile playing on his lips.

"Sure thing," I replied, handing it over with a sense of peace that had been absent for so long.

After breakfast, we'd sit down with our Bibles. Michael was hesitant at first, but I gently guided him through passages that had always given me strength.

"Let's read Psalm 23 today," I suggested one afternoon. "It's a reminder of God's unwavering presence."

Michael nodded and began to read aloud. As he did, I saw a spark of hope reignite in his eyes.

"The Lord is my shepherd; I shall not want," he read slowly, savoring each word. "He makes me lie down in green pastures. He leads me beside still waters."

I watched him closely, praying silently for these words to take root in his heart.

As we delved deeper into our studies, Michael started to open up more about his struggles and temptations. It wasn't easy for him, but I listened with an open heart.

"Mom, sometimes I still feel the pull to go back to my old ways," he admitted one evening as we sat at the kitchen table.

"I understand," I said gently but firmly. "Temptation is always there, but remember that God gives us the strength to resist."

We discussed practical steps he could take to stay on the right path—avoiding certain places and people, filling his time with positive activities.

"I've been thinking about joining a Bible study group at church," Michael said hesitantly one day. "Do you think that's a good idea?"

"I think it's a wonderful idea," I replied with a warm smile. "It will give you a support system and help you grow in your faith."

Through it all, I balanced nurturing advice with firm boundaries. When Michael expressed interest in going out with friends who had previously led him astray, I stood my ground.

"I'm proud of how far you've come," I told him seriously. "But it's important to protect your progress. Surround yourself with people who uplift you."

He nodded thoughtfully, understanding the wisdom in my words.

With each shared meal and heartfelt conversation, we slowly but surely rebuilt our fractured relationship. The road ahead was still long and challenging, but we faced it together—with love and unwavering faith as our guideposts.

Michael's transformation didn't just affect me; it began to ripple through our entire family. One evening, he asked if he could share his story with his siblings. We gathered in the living room, the cozy warmth of the fireplace flickering softly. Jessica and Ethan sat on the couch, their curiosity piqued.

"Guys, I want to talk to you about something important," Michael began, his voice steady yet humble. "I've been through a lot these past few years, and I've made some pretty bad choices. But I want you to know that I've found my way back to God."

Jessica crossed her arms, her face a mixture of skepticism and interest. Ethan leaned forward, eyes wide with anticipation.

"I got caught up in things that seemed fun at the time but only led me down a dark path," Michael continued. "I pushed away our parents and made them worry constantly. It wasn't until I hit rock bottom that I realized how much I needed God and our family."

Jessica's tough exterior began to soften as Michael spoke from his heart.

"I know I hurt all of you," Michael said, looking each of them in the eye. "And I'm truly sorry for that. But I want you to know it's never too late to turn things around."

Ethan shifted uncomfortably but couldn't hide the glimmer of hope in his eyes.

"Michael," he finally said, breaking the silence. "Do you really believe things can change? That we can change?"

"Yes, Ethan," Michael replied with conviction. "If God can turn my life around, He can do the same for you."

Jessica uncrossed her arms and sighed deeply. "I've been hanging out with people who aren't good for me," she admitted quietly. "Maybe it's time for a change."

Hearing her words felt like a breakthrough moment.

"That's a brave first step, Jess," I said gently.

In the days that followed, I saw subtle but significant shifts in both Jessica and Ethan. Jessica started distancing herself from her old friend group, choosing instead to spend more time at home or with positive influences at church. She even joined a youth Bible study group.

Ethan, inspired by Michael's transformation, began taking more interest in our family devotions and was more open to discussing his own struggles.

One afternoon, as we sat around the kitchen table doing homework and chatting, Jessica looked up at Michael.

"I'm proud of you," she said softly.

Michael smiled, gratitude shining in his eyes.

The tide was turning in our home—one step at a time—fueled by faith and the undeniable power of God's grace working through us all.

Seeing the change in Michael and its impact on Jessica and Ethan, I couldn't help but reflect on those agonizing years of discipline. The long nights spent in prayer, the constant worry, the endless battles over rules and standards—all of it now seemed to have been worth it. I thought about John 15:2, where Jesus talks about the necessity of pruning to bear more fruit. At times, being a mother felt like being a gardener, constantly cutting away at what seemed healthy to ensure future growth.

Those moments when I had to say no to Michael's requests to hang out with friends who were a bad influence, or when I insisted Jessica change her outfit before leaving the house—they were painful for all of us. I remembered the tearful arguments and slammed doors. I recalled how each act of discipline felt like an act of betrayal in their eyes.

But now, looking at my children gathered around the table, their hearts slowly turning back to what truly matters, I understood the wisdom of pruning. The small branches we cut away—Michael's rebellious friends, Jessica's immodest clothing choices—were necessary sacrifices for the health of the entire tree.

I glanced over at John as he helped Ethan with his math homework. His patience and steadfast support had been my rock through those difficult years. We had our share of disagreements, but he always stood by my side when it came to maintaining our family's biblical standards.

The momentary pains we endured are now overshadowed by the harvest we're beginning to see. The joy in Michael's eyes as he spoke about his renewed faith was a testament to that. Jessica's willingness to change her social circle and Ethan's growing interest in our family devotions were signs that our efforts weren't in vain.

I took a deep breath, feeling a wave of gratitude wash over me. The struggles and sacrifices seemed so small compared to the peace and unity slowly blossoming in our home. God had been faithful through it all, guiding us even when we felt lost.

As we sat there, sharing stories and laughing together, I realized that this was the harvest I had prayed for—a family rooted in faith, love, and mutual respect. The years of pruning had borne fruit far sweeter than any temporary comfort could have provided. And for that, I was profoundly grateful.

We sat around the kitchen table, the air thick with a blend of relief and unspoken gratitude. Michael was the first to break the silence.

"I never thought I'd say this," he began, looking directly at me, "but all those rules you laid down, they saved me. I hated them then, but now I see how they kept me from going too far off the deep end."

Jessica nodded in agreement. "I remember thinking you were just trying to ruin my life," she said, her voice tinged with remorse. "But those boundaries? They were like guardrails keeping me from completely derailing."

Ethan, usually quiet and observant, spoke up next. "I used to think you were just being mean, Mom. But now I get it. You wanted us to be safe and grounded."

Their words pierced through me, a mixture of pain and healing. It was as if all the years of struggling had culminated in this moment of clarity.

"I didn't understand then either," I admitted, my voice trembling. "I was so focused on doing what I thought was right that I sometimes forgot to show you why it mattered."

Michael leaned back in his chair, a thoughtful expression crossing his face. "I've gained an unshakable testimony because of those tough years," he said. "I wandered, but I found my way back to truth."

Jessica added softly, "Me too. I know now that real freedom comes from living within God's guidelines, not outside them."

Ethan looked at his siblings and then at me. "And I've learned that being grounded in faith makes you stronger than any peer pressure or temptation out there."

Their confessions filled me with a sense of awe and humility.

"I've changed too," I said quietly. "I used to think being a good mother meant enforcing rules without exception. But I've learned that wisdom sometimes means bending without breaking."

John squeezed my hand under the table, offering silent support.

"I've become humbler through all this," I continued. "Realizing that sometimes my sternness was more about my fears than your actions helped me become more empathetic."

The kids listened intently as I shared my own transformation.

"Being in the furnace has refined me as well," I said finally. "I've learned that love and discipline are not mutually exclusive; they must go hand in hand."

We sat there for a moment longer, soaking in the mutual understanding that had been so hard-won.

In that quiet kitchen, we found a new level of connection—one forged through fire but strengthened by faith.

Sunday morning, the sun filtered through the stained-glass windows of our small church, casting vibrant colors across the pews. We sat together as a family, shoulder to shoulder, a sight that had once seemed impossible. Michael on my left, Ethan on my right, and Jessica nestled between John and me. The pastor spoke about grace and redemption, words that resonated deeply with each of us.

Michael leaned over, whispering in my ear, "Remember when I used to say this was all 'lame'? Guess I was the lame one."

I chuckled softly, squeezing his hand. Jessica rolled her eyes playfully but smiled. Ethan nudged me with his elbow and whispered, "Bet you never thought you'd see us all here together like this."

"Not in a million years," I replied, my heart swelling with gratitude.

Later that day, we gathered around the dinner table for one of our boisterous family meals. The aroma of roasted chicken and freshly baked bread filled the air. John carved the bird while Jessica set out plates, her eyes twinkling as she recounted a funny story from school.

"Mom," she said between laughs, "remember that time you tried to teach me to cook spaghetti? And I ended up burning the water?"

We all burst into laughter, the sound filling the room with warmth. Michael added his own spin on the tale, embellishing details for comedic effect. Ethan chimed in with his own inside joke about my tendency to hide veggies in their meals when they were younger.

John raised his glass of iced tea. "To family," he said, his voice thick with emotion. "And to the love and grace that kept us bound together."

We clinked glasses, the simple act symbolizing so much more—our struggles, our reconciliations, our unwavering bond.

After dinner, we moved to the living room. Michael strummed a few chords on his guitar while Jessica and

Ethan bickered good-naturedly over what movie to watch. John settled into his armchair with a satisfied sigh.

I looked around at my family—united not just by blood but by faith and resilience. The road had been long and fraught with challenges, but here we were, stronger than ever. The joy of our communion filled me with an indescribable peace.

In those moments—sitting together in church, sharing inside jokes over dinner—I realized that love had always been our anchor. Through every trial and triumph, it was love that had kept us bound even when strained.

And it was love that would carry us forward into whatever came next.

I sat on the porch, watching my grandchildren play in the yard. Their laughter filled the air, mingling with the scent of freshly cut grass. Michael's son, Noah, was teaching his younger cousins how to catch a football. I smiled, thinking how much he resembled his father at that age—full of energy and a natural leader.

Jessica emerged from the house, balancing a tray of lemonade and cookies. She called out to her daughter, Lily, who was trying to climb the oak tree in the corner of the yard.

"Lily! Remember what we talked about? Be careful up there!"

Lily grinned and waved, but obediently came down. Jessica caught my eye and shrugged with a knowing smile. "Kids," she said, shaking her head.

I nodded, feeling a deep sense of satisfaction. It was like looking through a mirror into the past. Jessica had been just as adventurous and headstrong as Lily.

Ethan walked up, his toddler son in his arms. "Hey Mom," he said, sitting beside me on the porch swing. "Can you believe how big they're getting?"

"It's incredible," I replied, reaching out to tickle little Jonah under his chin. He giggled, wriggling in Ethan's arms.

Watching my children parent their own kids filled me with a profound sense of fulfillment. They had taken those biblical values John and I had instilled in them and were now passing them on to another generation. It wasn't always easy; I could see Jessica's struggle to balance discipline with love or Ethan's occasional frustration when Jonah threw a tantrum.

But they were committed. I saw it in the way Michael led family devotions every evening with Noah and his siblings, or how Jessica insisted on modesty and respect in her home despite societal pressures. Ethan often sought my advice on parenting challenges, reminding me so much of myself when I was young and unsure.

A commotion drew my attention back to the yard. Noah had climbed onto a makeshift stage—an overturned crate—and was pretending to preach a sermon, mimicking our pastor's gestures with uncanny accuracy.

Michael joined me on the porch, chuckling at his son's antics. "He's got quite the imagination," he said.

"Just like you did," I replied, patting his arm.

He looked at me seriously for a moment. "Thanks for everything, Mom," he said quietly. "For sticking to your guns even when we made it hard."

I squeezed his hand, tears pricking my eyes. "It was worth it," I whispered.

As I watched my grandchildren chase each other around the yard, I felt an overwhelming sense of peace. The seeds we had planted were bearing fruit—not just in our children but now in their children as well.

And that legacy? It was beautiful beyond words.

As I watched Noah continue his spirited sermon, the memory of that teenage outburst resurfaced. "You're not my friend, you're my mother!" Michael had spat those words at me with such venom. At the time, it felt like a knife to my heart. But now, seeing him here, a grown man with his own family, the weight of that moment had transformed.

Michael shifted on the porch swing beside me, catching my reflective gaze. "I remember saying that to you once," he began, his voice tinged with regret. "I didn't get it back then."

I turned to him, feeling the years melt away. "You were frustrated," I said gently. "And I understand why."

He shook his head. "No, I was wrong. You were right. You weren't just trying to be our friend; you were our mother—our spiritual guide." His eyes met mine, full of an understanding that had taken decades to form.

"When you told me that you weren't my friend but my mother, it stung because I didn't see the bigger picture," he continued. "But now, raising Noah and his siblings... I get it. You were building something deeper than friendship."

I felt tears welling up as I listened to him articulate what had been in my heart all those years. "It wasn't easy," I admitted. "There were times I questioned myself, wondering if I was too harsh or too strict."

Michael nodded. "But those standards you held us to—they shaped us. They grounded us in faith and principles that we're now passing on to our own kids."

Jessica walked over with Lily by her side, overhearing the conversation. "What are you two talking about?" she asked with a curious smile.

"Just reminiscing," Michael replied, sharing a look with her.

Jessica's face softened as she joined us on the porch steps. "You know, Mom," she said thoughtfully, "I used to think you were too strict too. But looking back...you were protecting us from so much we couldn't see."

I reached out and took both their hands in mine. "I did what I believed God called me to do—to be your mother first and foremost."

Ethan came up with Jonah still in his arms and heard Jessica's words. He smiled at me warmly and added, "And because of that, we're able to raise our kids with those same values."

My heart swelled as I looked at my children—now parents themselves—finally grasping the depth of my love and commitment. It made every battle worth fighting.

Noah's voice carried over from the yard, ending his sermon with an enthusiastic "Amen!" The children erupted in giggles and applause.

Michael leaned in close and whispered, "Thank you for being our mother first."

Chapter 7

Letting Go

A s Michael packed the last of his belongings into the car, my heart felt like it was being pulled in a thousand directions. I had spent years carefully sheltering him, guarding his heart and mind against the secular world's influences. Now, as he prepared to leave for college, I faced the terrifying reality that my guidance would no longer be a constant in his life.

"Mom, you're fussing again," Michael said with a half-smile as he caught me rearranging his neatly packed suitcase.

"I just want to make sure you have everything," I replied, forcing a smile of my own. Inside, a storm of anxiety brewed.

What if all the training we had poured into him unraveled under the pressures and temptations of college life? The world out there was vast and unyielding, filled with ideologies and influences that stood in stark contrast to the values we had instilled in him. Would he remember to cling to his faith when faced with newfound freedoms?

I couldn't help but voice my concern. "Michael, you know how important it is to stay grounded in your faith, right? College will bring so many new challenges."

He paused from his packing and looked at me earnestly. "Mom, I know. You've taught me well. I promise I'll stay true to what you and Dad have taught us."

His reassurance brought a fleeting moment of peace, but doubt quickly crept back in. What if peer pressure proved too strong? What if the secular ideologies he would encounter swayed him away from his beliefs? The thought of him drifting away from God gnawed at me.

I reached out and placed a hand on his arm. "Just remember, Michael. Whenever you feel lost or overwhelmed, turn to Scripture. Turn to God."

He nodded solemnly, understanding the depth of my concern. "I will, Mom. I promise."

As we loaded the last box into the car, John joined us, placing a comforting hand on my shoulder. "He's ready," John said softly.

I nodded, though my heart wasn't fully convinced. Watching Michael drive away felt like releasing a piece of my soul into an unpredictable world. The tears welled up as I whispered a fervent prayer for protection over him.

The house felt emptier without Michael's presence—a stark reminder that he was now venturing into a world beyond our sheltering walls. All I could do was pray that the seeds we had sown would take deep root and flourish even in the face of adversity.

"God," I whispered through my tears, "please watch over my son."

The drive to Michael's college was filled with a heavy silence, punctuated only by the hum of the engine and the occasional sniffle from me. I tried to keep my composure, but the pit in my stomach grew with each passing mile.

When we finally arrived and parked in front of his dorm, I took a deep breath, willing myself to be strong. We hauled his belongings up to his room, which felt stark and empty compared to the warmth of home. The bare walls and sparse furniture made my heart ache; this was where my son would be living now.

I busied myself making up his bed one last time, smoothing out the sheets with care. Each tuck and fold felt like a small act of love, a way to hold on just a little bit longer. Michael laughed as he unpacked, already chattering about the new friends he hoped to make and the activities he planned to join.

"Mom, you don't have to do that," he said, noticing my fussing over his bed.

"I know," I replied, forcing a smile. "But humor your old mom one last time."

He rolled his eyes playfully but let me continue. I could see the excitement bubbling in him, a stark contrast to the heaviness I felt.

Soon, there was a knock at the door—his roommate had arrived with his parents. The room instantly filled with chatter and introductions. Michael's eyes lit up as they started talking about their majors and upcoming orientation events.

I stood back, watching him blend seamlessly into this new world. He looked so grown-up, so ready for this next chapter of his life. The tears I had been holding back threatened to spill over, but I blinked them away, determined not to embarrass him.

"Michael," I called softly as he animatedly discussed weekend plans with his new friends.

He turned to me, his eyes full of excitement but also understanding. "I'll be fine, Mom."

I nodded, swallowing the lump in my throat. "I know you will be."

We hugged tightly, and for a moment, it felt like time stood still. Then he pulled away and turned back to his new life.

As John

When Michael walked through the door that first time he came home for break, my heart nearly stopped. His hair, once neatly trimmed, now hung shaggy and unruly. He wore a T-shirt with some band's logo I'd never seen before and jeans that were ripped at the knees. The Michael who stood before me looked nothing like the boy I had sent off to college just a few months prior.

"Hey, Mom," he greeted me casually, dropping his duffel bag in the hallway. "Good to be home."

I forced a smile, trying to mask my shock. "It's good to have you back," I replied, pulling him into a hug.

As we sat down for dinner, the changes in him became even more apparent. He talked about frat parties and co-ed dorms as if they were the most normal things in the world. My stomach churned as he mentioned a Halloween party where he and his friends dressed up in what sounded like wildly inappropriate costumes.

"And then there was this one girl who—" he started, but I cut him off.

"Michael, please," I said, unable to keep the tremor out of my voice. "Can we talk about something else?"

He looked at me, confused. "What's wrong, Mom? It's just college stuff."

Just college stuff. The words echoed in my mind like a warning bell. The immodesty and permissiveness of his new environment shook me to my core. The very things I had worked so hard to shield him from seemed to be swallowing him whole.

"I just... I wasn't expecting this," I managed to say.

Michael shrugged, seemingly oblivious to my inner turmoil. "You've got to lighten up a bit, Mom. It's not a big deal."

Not a big deal? The casual dismissal stung more than any outright rebellion ever could. My mind raced with images of all the influences now surrounding him—each one a potential threat to everything we had instilled in him over the years.

As he continued chatting about his new friends and campus life, I found it hard to concentrate on his words. All I could see was how drastically he had changed in such a short time. Each mention of another party or another instance of co-ed mingling felt like a blow to my carefully constructed beliefs.

I excused myself early from the table under the pretense of cleaning up in the kitchen. Standing over the sink with soapy water running over my hands, I silently prayed for strength and guidance.

I scrubbed the same plate over and over, lost in my thoughts. The soap bubbles popped, one by one, much like the bubble of control I had always tried to maintain. Michael was no longer the little boy I could guide with a firm hand and loving heart. He was an adult now, making his own choices, facing his own temptations. My heart ached with the realization that I couldn't protect him from everything.

"Mom?" Michael's voice broke through my reverie.

I turned to see him standing in the doorway, concern etched on his face. "Yes, Michael?"

"Are you okay? You seem... off."

I forced a smile. "Just thinking, that's all."

He stepped into the kitchen, leaning against the counter. "You know, I'm not a kid anymore. You don't have to worry so much."

The irony of his statement wasn't lost on me. Worrying was as natural to me as breathing. But he was right—he wasn't a child anymore. I had to trust that the seeds of faith we had planted would grow, even if they took root in rocky soil.

I remembered my own youth, the times I had strayed from the path my parents had set for me. There were moments when I too had wandered far from God's teachings before rededicating myself fully. Those memories brought a small measure of comfort. If God could bring me back from my wayward ways, surely He could do the same for Michael.

"I know you're not a kid," I said softly, placing the plate on the drying rack. "It's just hard to let go."

Michael's eyes softened. "I get it, Mom. But you've taught me well. More than you probably realize."

His words hit me like a gentle breeze on a hot day—refreshing and unexpectedly soothing. Maybe I needed to let go and trust that God would watch over him now.

"Thank you for saying that," I replied, feeling some of my anxiety melt away.

Michael smiled and gave me a quick hug before heading back to join his siblings in the living room. As I stood there in the kitchen, alone with my thoughts once more, I felt a strange sense of peace settle over me.

Trusting God with Michael's future meant relinquishing my grip and believing that those seeds of faith would sprout in their own time, according to His plan, not mine.

I finished washing up and joined my family in the living room, where laughter filled the air—a reminder that love and faith were still very much alive in our home.

The turkey's aroma filled the house, mingling with the scent of freshly baked pies. I glanced at the clock. Michael should be arriving any minute now. My heart fluttered with a mix of excitement and anxiety. It had been months since he'd been home, and I longed for a glimpse of the boy I used to know.

The door creaked open, and Michael walked in, lugging a suitcase behind him. He was taller, broader—more man than boy now. But something else had changed too. There was a hardness in his eyes that hadn't been there before.

"Michael! It's so good to see you," I exclaimed, wrapping him in a tight hug.

"Hey, Mom," he replied, his voice muffled against my shoulder. He pulled away and glanced around the room. "Where's everyone?"

"In the living room. They're watching a Christmas movie."

He nodded and started to head that way, but I couldn't help myself. "So, how are things? How's school? And... your girlfriend?"

He stiffened slightly but kept walking. "Everything's fine."

"Fine?" I pressed, following him into the living room. "You know you can talk to me about anything, right?"

He turned sharply to face me. "Mom, can we not do this right now?"

I felt a familiar pang in my chest—the one that comes from seeing your child pull away. But I had to ask; it was my duty as his mother.

"It's just that... I worry about you, Michael. Especially when it comes to your relationship with Jessica."

His jaw tightened. "What about Jessica?"

"Well," I hesitated, choosing my words carefully, "I've heard some things—about her beliefs, her lifestyle choices—that concern me."

He scoffed and shook his head. "Of course you have."

I reached out to touch his arm but he stepped back. "Michael, I'm just worried about you making choices that go against what we've taught you—about premarital relations and other things."

His eyes flashed with anger. "This again? You're always on about how everyone should live according to your rules."

"They're not just my rules; they're biblical principles," I countered, feeling my voice rise despite my efforts to stay calm.

"Biblical principles," he repeated mockingly. "Maybe they worked for you and Dad, but times are different now."

"God's Word doesn't change with time," I shot back.

He threw his hands up in exasperation. "This is why I hate coming home! You can't accept that I'm an adult making my own decisions."

The room fell silent except for the faint sound of the movie playing in the background. The distance between us felt insurmountable at that moment—like an ocean of misunderstandings and unmet expectations.

"We love you, Michael," I whispered, my voice breaking.

His expression softened for

The days following Michael's return home were tense. Every conversation felt like walking a tightrope, balancing between concern and respect for his newfound independence. It was clear that the dynamics had shifted, and I needed to find a new approach to guide him without pushing him further away.

One morning, as I stood at the kitchen counter making breakfast, Michael shuffled in, still groggy from sleep. He grabbed a mug and poured himself some coffee.

"Morning," I greeted, trying to keep my tone light.

"Morning," he mumbled back.

I watched him for a moment, searching for the right words. "You know, Michael, I've been thinking... I understand that things are different now that you're in college."

He looked up, wary. "Yeah?"

"Yes," I continued, choosing my words carefully. "And I realize that you need some freedoms to figure things out on your own. But there are certain behaviors that I can't allow under this roof."

He sighed and leaned against the counter. "Like what?"

"Like bringing Jessica here overnight," I said gently. "It's important to uphold our family's values at home."

His eyes narrowed slightly but he didn't interrupt.

"I'm not saying you can't see her," I added quickly. "Just... not here. You understand?"

He took a sip of his coffee, thinking it over. "So you're saying it's fine if I stay over at her place?"

I hesitated but nodded slowly. "As much as it pains me, yes. I can't control everything outside these walls. But under this roof, we have certain standards."

Michael nodded, his expression thoughtful rather than rebellious for once. "Alright, Mom. I get it."

Relief washed over me as he accepted the compromise without further argument.

Later that day, we found ourselves in another delicate situation when Jessica came over for dinner. She was wearing a crop top that left little to the imagination.

"Jessica," I began gently after pulling her aside into the hallway, "we have a modesty policy in our home."

She blinked at me, confused.

"I'm not asking you to change who you are," I explained, trying to be diplomatic. "But could you wear something a bit more... covered when you're here? It's just out of respect for our family's beliefs."

She nodded slowly and went upstairs to borrow one of Jessica's old sweaters without much fuss.

Finding this balance wasn't easy—it felt like navigating a minefield at times—but it was necessary. It allowed me to uphold our family's principles without coming across as too harsh or inflexible in this new phase of our lives.

As the days passed, I realized that my role as Michael's mother had to shift. He was no longer the boy who needed me to dictate his every move. Now, I had to become more of an advisor, someone he could turn to for guidance rather than rigid rules.

One evening after dinner, I called Michael into the living room. He sat on the edge of the couch, his eyes questioning.

"I've been thinking," I began, "about how you're adjusting to college life and everything that comes with it."

He nodded slowly, waiting for me to continue.

"I know it's not easy," I said. "You're navigating a lot of new experiences and freedoms. But I also know you need support from people other than just your family."

He looked puzzled. "What do you mean?"

"I mean connecting you with some youth pastors and mentors at your new church," I explained. "People who can offer guidance and be there for you in ways that might be different from how I can."

Michael's eyes widened a bit, but he didn't interrupt.

"I've already reached out to Pastor Steve," I continued. "He's willing to meet with you and introduce you to some of the young adult leaders in the congregation."

Michael leaned back, absorbing what I'd said. "You think that'll help?"

"I do," I replied firmly. "Sometimes we need outside perspectives, people who understand our struggles but aren't directly involved in our lives. They can offer wisdom and support in ways that family might not be able to."

He nodded again, more assured this time. "Alright, Mom. I'll give it a shot."

The next Sunday, we attended a service at Michael's new church together. Afterward, Pastor Steve greeted us warmly and introduced Michael to a few young men who led small groups and youth activities.

"This is David," Pastor Steve said, gesturing toward a tall young man with an easy smile. "He's one of our young adult leaders and a great mentor."

David extended his hand toward Michael. "Nice to meet you, man. Heard a lot about you from your mom."

Michael shook his hand and smiled back, albeit a bit shyly.

"Why don't you join us for our small group meeting this Wednesday?" David suggested. "We'd love to have you."

Michael glanced at me for a moment before nodding. "Yeah, sounds good."

As we drove home, I felt a sense of peace settle over me. By placing Michael's spiritual care in the hands of these mentors, I was completing what I'd started years ago—ensuring he had the guidance he needed even as he ventured into adulthood.

Weeks passed, and Michael began attending the small group meetings regularly. Each time he returned home, there was a subtle shift in his demeanor—an assurance that warmed my heart.

One Friday evening, he sat down at the kitchen table, his eyes meeting mine with a steadiness I hadn't seen in a while.

"Mom," he began, "I had a conversation with Emily today."

Emily was his girlfriend, someone I had been worried about. Their relationship seemed too intense too quickly, something that always set off alarm bells in my mind.

"Oh?" I tried to keep my tone neutral, though my curiosity piqued.

"Yeah," he said, taking a deep breath. "We talked about boundaries. I told her that I wanted to take things slower and focus on our spiritual growth together."

A flood of relief washed over me. "How did she take it?"

"Surprisingly well," he admitted. "She respected it and agreed we should be more mindful of our actions."

I couldn't hide my smile. "Michael, that's wonderful."

He shrugged but couldn't conceal the pride in his eyes. "It's just... everything you and Dad taught me, it's starting to make sense now."

Later that week, another moment reinforced that the foundation we laid still held firm. Michael came home from one of his small group meetings visibly animated.

"Mom," he said as soon as he walked through the door, "you won't believe what happened today."

"What is it?" I asked, setting aside the book I was reading.

"We had this discussion about faith and science," he began. "One of the guys in the group started questioning if you could believe in both."

"And?" I leaned in, eager to hear more.

"And I told them you can. I shared how you always taught us that faith and reason aren't enemies but allies."

His words brought tears to my eyes. All those years of discussions around the dinner table, the Bible studies we had—it all came rushing back.

"That's incredible, Michael," I said softly.

He nodded, a determined look crossing his face. "It felt good to stand up for what I believe."

In those moments—whether it was setting boundaries with Emily or defending his faith among peers—I saw the fruits of our labor. The tough love and unwavering standards weren't for nothing. They had produced an anchor for him amidst life's storms.

As I watched Michael walk away, heading toward his room with a newfound confidence, my heart swelled with gratitude. God had indeed been faithful through it all.

I found myself in constant prayer, my heart a sanctuary of hope and intercession. Michael had come so far, yet the road ahead still held countless unknowns. As he navigated his own path, I knew the time had come to pass the baton. But even from afar, I would always be his spiritual mother.

"Lord, guide him," I whispered while washing dishes one evening. The suds clung to my hands as I scrubbed away the remnants of dinner, but my mind was fixed on Michael's journey. "Give him strength and wisdom to stand firm."

Each time he left for his small group meetings, I felt a pang of worry mixed with pride. I had to trust that the seeds we planted over the years would bear fruit. He was no longer just my boy; he was a young man making choices of eternal significance.

One afternoon, as I folded laundry, Michael came home and sat at the edge of the couch.

"Mom," he said, his voice filled with an urgency that caught my attention.

I turned to face him, sensing another pivotal moment. "What is it, Michael?"

"We talked about integrity today," he began, eyes earnest. "How it's not just about what you do when people are watching but when they're not."

I nodded, feeling the weight of his words sink in. "And what did you share?"

"I told them about Dad's example," he said quietly. "How he always emphasized doing the right thing even when it's hard."

Tears welled up in my eyes. "That's true integrity."

He looked at me with a depth of understanding that reassured me more than any words could.

As I lay in bed that night, listening to the rhythmic breathing of John beside me, I continued my silent prayers for Michael. "Father, let him walk closely with You," I pleaded. "Protect his heart and mind."

Though miles might one day separate us physically, spiritually I would never stop mothering him. Every verse we read together, every prayer we uttered as a family—those moments had crafted an invisible tether binding us together through faith.

Michael's journey was his own now, but my role wasn't entirely over. It had simply evolved. From a distance or up close, through prayer or direct conversation, I would continue to guide him as best as I could.

"He's in Your hands now," I whispered into the stillness of our bedroom. "Thank You for letting me be his mother."

Chapter 8

Steadying the Ship

I stood in the quiet kitchen, the morning light filtering through the curtains. The stillness felt foreign. The house, once bursting with noise and activity, now echoed with silence. Michael, Jessica, and Ethan had all flown the nest, leaving behind an emptiness I hadn't anticipated.

I missed the chaos of breakfast routines, the hurried prayers before school, even the arguments over who got the last piece of toast. Now, each day began in solitude. I no longer could control their environments or enforce our household rules. It was a strange new reality, one I struggled to accept.

I found myself reaching for my phone multiple times a day, itching to call them, to check in on their lives. But I resisted. They needed space to grow, to make their own choices—even if those choices sometimes worried me.

As I stood by the window, watching the leaves rustle in the breeze, a pang of longing gripped my heart. I remembered how I used to monitor their every move—ensuring they followed curfews, kept up with their studies, attended youth group. Now, I had no oversight into their daily lives. Were they keeping up with their faith? Making wise decisions? Avoiding harmful influences?

"Lord," I whispered into the quiet room, "watch over them where I cannot."

It was hard to relinquish control. Harder still to trust that the values John and I had instilled would guide them now that they were beyond our reach. Jessica's newfound independence concerned me the most; she had always pushed boundaries more than her brothers.

Sitting down at the kitchen table, I opened my Bible to Psalm 121. "The Lord will watch over your coming and going both now and forevermore," it read. A small comfort in my sea of worries.

John found me there later, deep in thought. He placed a gentle hand on my shoulder.

"They'll be okay," he said quietly.

"I hope so," I replied, my voice thick with emotion. "It's just so hard not knowing what they're doing every day."

"We raised them well," he reassured me. "We have to trust that."

I nodded but couldn't shake the unease gnawing at me. Each of our children faced a world full of temptations and trials without our immediate guidance or protection.

All I could do now was pray and hope that God's hand would continue to lead them as they ventured out into life on their own.

Jessica's phone call had come like a thunderclap.

"Mom, I'm moving in with Kyle," she declared, her voice defiant but with an undertone of uncertainty.

My heart sank. Kyle wasn't just a boyfriend; he represented everything John and I had tried to shield her from. He didn't share our faith, had no respect for our values, and his lifestyle was a glaring contradiction to everything we'd taught her.

"Jessica, you know what we believe about living together before marriage," I responded, trying to keep my voice steady. "It's not just about rules; it's about honoring God."

"I'm an adult now, Mom," she retorted. "I need to live my life, make my own choices."

After hanging up, I sat in stunned silence, clutching the phone. My firstborn daughter was slipping through my fingers, embracing a world that I had fought so hard to keep at bay. The thought of her salary being squandered on parties and superficial pleasures made my stomach churn.

John found me in the kitchen later that evening. "What's wrong?" he asked, concern etched on his face.

"Jessica's moving in with Kyle," I whispered, tears welling up. "I don't know how much more I can take."

He sighed deeply and wrapped his arms around me. "We have to trust God with her," he said softly. "We've done all we can."

But it didn't feel like enough. Every fiber of my being screamed to intervene, to pull her back from the precipice she was teetering on. Yet another part of me knew that sometimes, the hardest lessons were learned through experience.

The next few weeks were torture. Jessica's social media posts were filled with images of parties and outings that made my heart ache. The carefree smile on her face contrasted sharply with the turmoil I felt inside.

One Sunday afternoon, as John and I sat on the porch after church, he looked at me with a mixture of sadness and resolve. "Sarah, maybe she needs to hit rock bottom before she can find her way back."

His words echoed my own internal struggle. How much could I intervene without pushing her further away? How could I stand by and watch her make choices that led her down such a dangerous path?

"God, give me wisdom," I prayed silently, feeling more helpless than ever before.

Jessica was out there living a life so far removed from the one we'd envisioned for her. All we could do now was pray fervently for her protection and eventual return to the faith that once grounded her so firmly in our family's values.

The agony of watching Jessica freefall was almost unbearable, but perhaps John was right—sometimes the hardest lessons are the ones learned through fire.

I could see it in his eyes—the confusion, the doubt. Ethan, my youngest, had always been the most passionate about his faith. From the time he was a child, he'd absorbed every Bible story, memorized every verse. But now, something had shifted.

It started subtly at first. He'd come home from college and make offhand comments about things his professors said. "Mom, did you know there are other accounts of creation myths in different cultures?" he'd ask, trying to sound casual but with an undercurrent of something deeper.

One evening, as we sat around the dinner table, Ethan pushed his food around on his plate, his mind clearly elsewhere.

"What's on your mind?" I asked gently.

"Mom," he began hesitantly, "how do we know that what we believe is really the truth? I mean, what makes Christianity different from all those other religions?"

The question pierced me. This was more than academic curiosity; it was the beginning of a crisis I had hoped my children would never face.

"Ethan," I said slowly, choosing my words with care, "our faith isn't just about knowledge or tradition. It's about a relationship with God. It's about experiencing His love and grace."

He sighed deeply and looked down. "But what if... what if that relationship is just something we've been taught to feel? My professors say there's no empirical evidence for any of it."

My heart ached hearing this. The seed of doubt had been planted, and it was being watered by every skeptical peer and professor he encountered.

Days turned into weeks, and Ethan grew more distant. He started skipping church services, opting instead to spend time in his room reading books on philosophy and science. Each new argument he encountered seemed to chip away at the foundation I had so diligently tried to build.

One night, he came home late and found me in the living room reading my Bible. His eyes were red-rimmed, whether from exhaustion or tears I couldn't tell.

"Mom," he said quietly as he sank into the chair opposite me, "I don't know what to believe anymore."

His admission felt like a knife twisting in my heart. This was my baby—the one who had once clung to every word of Scripture with unwavering faith. Now he stood on shaky ground, questioning everything I had taught him since childhood.

As much as I wanted to fix it for him, I knew this was a journey Ethan had to navigate on his own. My role now was to love him through it and pray that God would lead him back to solid ground.

Michael sat at the kitchen table, his eyes glued to his phone. The familiar glow illuminated his face, but what troubled me more were the words that came out of his mouth. He was home for the weekend, and I had hoped for meaningful conversations. Instead, he filled the air with comments that made my heart sink.

"Mom, have you ever considered that maybe we're too strict on some of these social issues?" Michael's tone was casual, but his words cut deep.

I put down the dish I was drying and turned to face him. "What do you mean?"

"Take politics, for example," he continued. "I think some of the policies you support are outdated. We need to be more progressive, more accepting of different lifestyles."

His comments left me speechless for a moment. This wasn't the Michael I had raised—the one who once passionately defended biblical principles in youth group debates.

"Michael, our beliefs are rooted in Scripture," I said slowly. "They're not just about being 'progressive' or 'conservative.' They're about living according to God's Word."

He shrugged, barely looking up from his phone. "I know, Mom. But times are changing. We have to adapt or we'll be left behind."

The words felt like a slap in the face. Adapt? Left behind? These were not the values I had instilled in him. My mind raced back to all those years of family devotions, Bible studies, and heartfelt prayers.

"And what about materialism?" I pressed on, not ready to let this go. "How does that fit into your new 'progressive' worldview?"

Michael finally looked up, a hint of annoyance in his eyes. "There's nothing wrong with wanting nice things, Mom. It's called enjoying life."

"But Jesus taught us to store treasures in heaven, not on earth," I countered.

He sighed heavily and stood up from the table. "Mom, you're always going on about this stuff. Can't we just agree to disagree?"

As he walked away, I felt a wave of despair wash over me. Michael still attended church when he was home; he still spoke Christianese fluently enough to fool most people. But beneath that veneer of faith lay a heart that had drifted far from its anchor.

His comments about politics and social issues were troubling enough, but it was his casual acceptance of materialism that cut me the deepest. It wasn't just about wanting nice things—it was about a fundamental shift in values that seemed irreconcilable with the faith we had once shared so deeply.

My heart ached as I watched him retreat into another room, his phone still casting its glow onto his face. How had we come to this place? And how could we find our way back?

I took a deep breath, steeling myself for the conversation ahead. Ethan had always been the quiet one, my baby who grew up to be a man of conviction. But his latest conviction had sent ripples of worry through my heart. He had met someone—someone wonderful, he assured me—but she wasn't a believer.

"Mom," Ethan's voice broke through my thoughts as he walked into the kitchen. "Can we talk?"

"Of course, Ethan," I replied, putting down the dishcloth and sitting across from him at the table. "What's on your mind?"

He hesitated, fiddling with his hands. "It's about Sarah."

The name alone made my heart tighten. I had prayed for Ethan's future spouse since he was born, and now here she was—a wonderful woman by all accounts, but missing the most crucial part of what I had prayed for: faith.

"Go on," I urged him gently.

"I know you have concerns about her not being a Christian," he started slowly. "But I love her, Mom. She's kind, thoughtful, and she respects our beliefs even if she doesn't share them."

I nodded, taking in his words but feeling the weight of what I had to say next. "Ethan, you know how much I care about you and your happiness. But marrying someone who doesn't share your faith—it's a big risk."

"I understand that," he said quickly. "But people change. She might come to faith later on."

"Might," I echoed softly. "But what if she doesn't? Marriage is hard enough when both partners share the same faith."

He looked at me with a mix of frustration and pleading in his eyes. "Are you saying you won't support us?"

I took another deep breath, knowing this would be one of the hardest things I'd ever say to my son. "Ethan, if you choose to marry Sarah without her coming to faith first, I can't attend your wedding."

The silence that followed was deafening.

"You can't be serious," he finally said, disbelief etched across his face.

"I am serious," I replied firmly but with a heavy heart. "I love you deeply, but there are some boundaries I cannot budge on."

He stood up abruptly, pushing his chair back with more force than necessary. "So that's it? You'd rather miss your own son's wedding than bend a little?"

Tears welled up in my eyes as I stood to face him. "Ethan, this isn't about bending; it's about holding firm to what we believe is true and right according to Scripture."

His face twisted in frustration and hurt as he stormed out of the kitchen, leaving me standing there alone with my tears and convictions.

Some boundaries are too crucial to cross, even when it breaks your heart to hold them firm.

As Ethan's footsteps faded down the hallway, I sank back into my chair, the weight of our conversation pressing down on me. The house felt emptier than ever. I knew Ethan loved Sarah deeply, and it tore at me to set such a hard line. But it wasn't the only battle I faced.

Choosing which battles to fight had become an art form over the years. With three grown children, each with their own personalities and paths, the gray areas seemed to multiply.

Take Michael, for instance. He had always been the most defiant, testing every boundary we set. When he came home from college sporting tattoos and piercings, I felt a pang of disappointment but knew it wasn't worth a nuclear feud. I bit my tongue, choosing instead to focus on our deeper conversations about faith and purpose.

And then there was Jessica. She had always been head-strong, pushing back against my rules about modesty and curfews. When she moved in with her boyfriend, it felt like a dagger to my heart. But I had to pick my battles carefully. If I lashed out at every transgression, I risked pushing her further away.

I remember one evening when Jessica came home late, her clothes reeking of smoke and alcohol. She stumbled through the door, and I was ready to unleash a torrent of reprimands. But as she collapsed on the couch, looking more like a lost little girl than a rebellious teenager, I paused.

"Jess," I began softly, sitting beside her.

She groaned in response, barely lifting her head.

"I'm worried about you," I continued, choosing my words carefully. "This path you're on—it's dangerous."

She looked up at me with bleary eyes but didn't argue.

"Just... promise me you'll be careful," I said finally.

It wasn't the stern lecture I wanted to give, but in that moment, it felt right to turn a blind eye toward the specifics and focus on keeping our lines of communication open.

The judgment calls never got easier. Every day seemed to bring a new challenge that required balancing conviction with compassion. As much as I wanted to control every aspect of their lives, they were adults now—free to make their own choices and mistakes.

My heart ached with each compromise, each moment when I chose silence over confrontation for the sake of preserving our fragile peace. It was a delicate dance between holding firm to biblical truths and knowing when to let go for love's sake.

Some days were easier than others. Some days... well, some days felt like defeat wrapped in grace.

Unable to be a constant presence, I sought out spiritual reinforcements. The weight of their choices and the limited control I had over their lives gnawed at me daily. One evening, after another restless night of prayer, I decided to call Pastor Thomas.

"Pastor, it's Sarah," I began, my voice betraying the exhaustion I felt.

"Sarah, how are you?" His voice was warm, a balm to my weary soul.

"I need your help," I confessed. "The kids... they're all going in different directions. I'm afraid I can't reach them like I used to."

There was a pause on the other end. "Tell me what's going on."

I poured out my heart—the struggles with Michael's wavering faith, Jessica's rebellion, and Ethan's crisis of belief. Pastor Thomas listened patiently, interjecting only to ask clarifying questions.

"We can set up regular check-ins with them," he suggested. "I know Michael has always connected well with Elder Williams. Maybe he can meet up with him?"

"That would be wonderful," I replied, feeling a glimmer of hope.

"And for Jessica," Pastor Thomas continued, "perhaps Sister Marlene could reach out. She's been through her own rebellious phase and might connect with her on a deeper level."

"Yes, Marlene could be just what Jess needs," I agreed.

"As for Ethan," Pastor Thomas said thoughtfully, "I can have some of our young adult leaders invite him to their Bible study group. Sometimes hearing from peers who've gone through similar struggles can make a difference."

T

I found myself in the living room, late at night, unable to sleep. The house was eerily quiet, the only sound the ticking of the clock on the mantel. I sank to my knees, feeling the weight of my burdens pressing down on me. My hands clenched into fists, and I raised them toward the heavens, my voice trembling with desperation.

"Lord," I began, my voice breaking, "please, hear me."

Tears streamed down my face as I poured out my heart. "Father, I am utterly broken. My children are lost, and I feel powerless to save them."

My fists shook as I continued, "Michael is drifting away from the faith we worked so hard to instill in him. Jessica... she's fallen into a life of rebellion that terrifies me. And Ethan... oh God, Ethan is questioning everything he's ever known."

I felt the anguish welling up inside me, threatening to consume me. "Please, Lord, don't let them slip away. Reach into their hearts and bring them back to You."

My voice grew louder, more raw with each word. "I've done everything I can! I've prayed, I've disciplined, I've loved them with all that I am. But it's not enough. I need You to intervene!"

I collapsed onto the floor, sobbing uncontrollably. "Lord, I can't do this alone. I need Your strength. I need Your wisdom. Show me how to reach them. Show me how to be the mother they need."

My cries echoed through the empty house as I pleaded with God for their souls. "Break through their stubbornness, their rebellion, their doubts. Fill them with Your Spirit and draw them back to You."

In that moment of utter despair, I felt a flicker of hope—a reminder that God's power was greater than my fears.

"Please," I whispered through my tears, "save my children."

As I knelt there, utterly spent, my phone rang, cutting through the silence. My heart skipped a beat. I wiped my eyes and fumbled to answer, the glow of the screen illuminating my tear-streaked face. It was Michael.

"Mom?" His voice sounded different—calmer, more introspective.

"Michael? Is everything okay?"

"I... I just wanted to tell you something," he began, hesitating. "I've been going to this campus ministry group. It's nothing like I expected. They're really genuine, you know? And... well, it's got me thinking."

My breath caught in my throat. "Thinking about what?"

"About everything you and Dad taught me," he admitted. "I've been feeling convicted about how I've been living. It's like... I can't ignore it anymore."

Tears welled up again, but this time they were tears of relief. "Michael, that's wonderful news. I'm so proud of you."

He chuckled softly, a sound that felt like a balm to my weary soul. "I just thought you should know."

"Thank you for telling me," I whispered, my voice thick with emotion. "Keep seeking God, Michael. He has great plans for you."

After we hung up, I stayed on the floor for a moment longer, feeling a sense of peace wash over me. It wasn't a complete resolution—far from it—but it was a glimmer of hope.

I rose slowly, my knees protesting after being on the hard floor for so long. As I walked through the quiet house, I whispered a prayer of gratitude.

"Thank You, Lord," I said softly. "Thank You for hearing me. Thank You for working in Michael's heart."

I knew there would still be challenges ahead. Jessica and Ethan's struggles weren't resolved overnight, and neither were Michael's. But that phone call was a reminder that God was still at work, even if His answers came slowly.

Back in my room, I knelt once more beside my bed.

"Father," I prayed, "thank You for this sign of hope. Help me to stay strong in faith and continue praying for my children with unwavering trust in Your timing."

As I lay down to rest, the heaviness in my heart lifted just a little. It wasn't an end to our struggles but rather a precious assurance that God was listening and moving in ways unseen.

And that was enough to keep me going another day.

Chapter 9

Full Circle

A s I sat by the window, sipping my morning coffee, I found myself lost in the circular nature of life and parenting. The years seemed to spiral back upon themselves, a never-ending loop of love, discipline, and faith. Just as my parents had raised me with unwavering principles, I now watched that cycle continue with my own children.

Michael called last week to share that he and his wife were expecting their first child. The news sent a rush of emotions flooding through me—a kaleidoscope of memories from when he was just a baby in my arms. I could almost feel the weight of him again, smell the faint scent of baby powder and hear his tiny giggles.

Jessica had recently confided in me about her own struggles with her spirited toddler, Lily. "Mom, how did you manage?" she asked one evening over the phone. Her voice wavered between exhaustion and admiration. "I feel like I'm failing every day."

I smiled to myself, remembering my own desperate calls to my mother when Michael was a toddler. "Just keep planting those seeds," I had told Jessica. "You might not see the fruit right away, but it's there, growing silently beneath the surface."

Ethan had taken a different path, traveling overseas with his young family to do mission work. He sent letters filled with stories of their adventures and challenges, each one reminding me of the values we instilled in him from an early age. Despite the distance, I felt a profound connection to him through our shared faith.

Looking back, I could see the hand of God weaving through every moment—the discipline that felt so harsh at times now bore fruit in the lives my children were building. Each decision made out of love and conviction was now being echoed in their parenting styles.

A soft knock on the door pulled me from my reverie. It was John, holding a letter from Michael in his hand.

"Another update from our soon-to-be grandparenting adventure," he said with a warm smile.

I took the letter, my heart swelling with gratitude for this new chapter unfolding before us. As I opened it and began to read, I marveled at how life had come full circle.

My parents' wisdom had been passed down through me and was now being lived out by Michael, Jessica, and Ethan. And so the cycle continued—a beautiful testament to God's enduring faithfulness through generations.

The morning sun streamed through the window, casting a golden glow on the kitchen table where so many prayers had been whispered and tears shed. It felt like a sacred space where past met present and future—all bound together by threads of faith and love.

And for that moment, it was enough.

I watched from the doorway as Michael sat on the edge of his son's bed, a well-worn Bible in his hands. The soft glow of the bedside lamp illuminated his face, revealing a gentleness that hadn't always been there during his teenage years. He turned the pages with a familiarity that spoke of years of practice, settling on a passage with a smile.

"Tonight, we're reading about David and Goliath," he said, his voice filled with warmth and enthusiasm.

His two young children, Caleb and Emma, snuggled under their blankets, eyes wide with anticipation. They leaned in closer as Michael began to read, his voice weaving the ancient story into their imaginations. He paused at the right moments, adding emphasis and excitement, making sure every word resonated with them.

"And David said to the Philistine, 'You come to me with a sword and with a spear and with a javelin, but I come to you in the name of the Lord of hosts,'" Michael read, glancing up to see Caleb's mouth form an astonished "O."

Emma's tiny fingers clutched her stuffed lamb tightly. "Daddy, was David scared?" she asked, her voice barely above a whisper.

Michael closed the Bible gently and placed it on the nightstand. "He might have been," he said thoughtfully. "But he trusted God more than he feared Goliath. That's what made him brave."

He leaned over to kiss each child on the forehead before they clasped their hands together for bedtime prayers. "Dear Lord," Michael began, "thank you for this day and for my wonderful children. Help us all to be brave like David and trust in You no matter what giants we face."

As I stood there, watching this tender moment unfold, I felt an overwhelming sense of gratitude. The very principles I had worked so hard to instill in Michael were now being passed down to another generation. It was as if all those years of discipline, prayer, and unwavering faith had culminated in this beautiful scene before me.

After tucking them in and turning off the light, Michael quietly left the room and joined me in the hallway.

"You're doing an amazing job," I whispered, my voice choked with emotion.

He smiled, wrapping an arm around my shoulders. "I learned from the best," he replied softly.

In that moment, I knew that every struggle had been worth it. Seeing my son actively passing down our faith brought me more joy than words could express.

As I watched Michael guide his children through their nightly prayers, my heart swelled with pride and relief. Yet, it wasn't long before my thoughts drifted to Jessica.

Jessica, my fiercely independent daughter, had always been the one to challenge our household rules. Now, as a mother herself, she outwardly professed her faith but took a different approach in raising her own children. Her home echoed with laughter and freedom that sometimes bordered on chaos. I often wondered if she remembered the principles we'd instilled in her.

I visited Jessica one afternoon, finding her in the backyard with her children, Grace and Tommy. They ran barefoot across the grass, their giggles filling the air. Jessica sat on a blanket, watching them with a relaxed smile.

"Hey Mom," she called out when she saw me, patting the space beside her.

I settled down next to her, trying to ignore the small knot of concern in my stomach. "They seem to be having fun," I commented.

"Oh, they're wild," Jessica laughed. "But I let them be kids. They need freedom to explore and learn on their own."

As Tommy darted past us, I noticed his T-shirt bore a slogan that made me inwardly wince—a far cry from the modest attire I had insisted on during her upbringing. Grace ran up to us, breathless and excited.

"Mommy, can we watch that new superhero movie tonight?" she asked eagerly.

Jessica nodded without hesitation. "Sure thing, sweetie."

I bit my tongue but couldn't help myself for long. "Isn't that movie a bit... mature for them?" I asked gently.

Jessica's smile faltered for a moment before she replied. "They're exposed to so much these days anyway, Mom. I'd rather they experience it with me around to explain things."

I nodded slowly but couldn't shake my unease. While Jessica's permissive style came from a place of love and trust, it contrasted sharply with the boundaries John and I had set for our own children. I worried about how this looser ethical framework might impact Grace and Tommy as they grew older.

We sat in silence for a while, watching the kids play. Jessica seemed content with her choices, but I couldn't ignore the nagging feeling that they might lead to unforeseen consequences down the road.

"Jessica," I began carefully, "I know you're doing what you think is best for them. Just remember how important it is to keep guiding them with faith."

She looked at me thoughtfully before nodding. "I know, Mom," she said softly. "I'll always make sure they know God's love."

Her words reassured me somewhat, but as I left her house that day, my heart remained heavy with concern for my grandchildren's spiritual upbringing.

One afternoon, I sat in Jessica's living room, watching Grace and Tommy play a video game. The colorful animations flashed on the screen, and the room buzzed with the sound of digital explosions. Jessica was in the kitchen, preparing snacks, when I heard Grace's voice rise sharply.

"I told you, Tommy! It's my turn!" she snapped, snatching the controller from her younger brother.

Tommy's face crumpled as he looked up at her. "But you've had it for an hour," he protested.

Jessica walked in, carrying a tray of sandwiches. "What's going on here?" she asked, setting the tray down.

Grace turned to her mother with a defiant glare. "Tommy won't let me play. He's being so annoying."

"Grace, share with your brother," Jessica said calmly.

"No! It's not fair!" Grace shouted, her small hands tightening around the controller.

I watched the scene unfold, my heart sinking. The stubbornness in Grace's eyes mirrored Jessica's at that age. It was like watching history repeat itself. I felt a pang of anxiety; would this cycle lead to the same battles we had faced years ago?

Jessica sighed and crouched down to Grace's level. "Sweetie, you need to take turns. That's how we play fair."

Grace huffed and crossed her arms. "But I don't want to! He always gets his way."

The defiance in her tone echoed Jessica's teenage years when she had fought against our rules and curfews. I felt an urge to step in, to say something that might diffuse the tension or offer guidance.

Instead, I stayed silent, unsure if my interjection would help or hinder the situation. Watching my granddaughter push back against her mother brought back memories of our own heated arguments over modesty and curfews.

Jessica took a deep breath and stood up. "Grace, you need to listen to me. Share with Tommy or you'll lose game privileges for the rest of the day."

Grace glared but reluctantly handed the controller to Tommy. She flopped onto the couch beside me, arms still crossed.

As Jessica returned to the kitchen, she cast a weary glance my way. Our eyes met briefly, and I saw a flicker of frustration mixed with determination in her gaze. She was handling it in her own way, just as I had once tried with her.

I wanted to reassure her that this phase would pass or offer advice from my own experiences. But instead, I sat quietly, torn between respecting Jessica's approach and my desire to protect Grace from making similar mistakes.

In that moment, I realized how hard it was to watch history unfold without stepping in. The urge to guide and correct was strong, yet this was Jessica's journey now—her chance to navigate motherhood just as I had done before her.

Sitting in the back pew of the small church, I marveled at the sight before me. Ethan stood at the pulpit, his voice steady and passionate as he spoke to the congregation. It was a youth service, and the pews were filled with teenagers, some of them looking as rebellious as he once did.

Ethan's transformation was nothing short of miraculous. He had gone from a confused young man questioning his faith to a beacon of hope and truth for these kids. As I watched him, I couldn't help but remember the dark days when I feared he might never return to the path we had laid out for him.

"Let me tell you something," Ethan said, his eyes scanning the room. "I've been where some of you are now—lost, questioning everything, feeling like no one understands you. But I'm here to tell you that God never gives up on us. His love is relentless."

A young girl in the front row wiped a tear from her cheek. The words resonated deeply with many in attendance, just as they did with me.

After the service, I found Ethan in his small office. The walls were adorned with posters of Christian bands and Bible verses scrawled on index cards.

"Mom," he greeted me warmly, wrapping me in a hug.

"I'm so proud of you," I whispered, feeling tears well up.

He pulled back and smiled. "It's all God's work, Mom. I'm just His vessel."

Just then, a middle-aged couple knocked on the door-frame hesitantly. Ethan waved them in.

"Come in, Mr. and Mrs. Davis," he said. "This is my mom."

They nodded at me before turning their attention back to Ethan. "We need your help," Mrs. Davis began, her voice trembling slightly. "Our son... he's going down a dark path."

Ethan nodded empathetically. "I understand," he said softly. "Let's pray together first."

We bowed our heads as Ethan led us in prayer, asking for wisdom and strength for this troubled family. When we finished, he looked at them with compassionate eyes.

"I've been where your son is," Ethan said gently. "But there's hope. God can turn any heart back to Him."

Mr. Davis looked visibly relieved while Mrs. Davis clung to his every word as if they were a lifeline.

Ethan continued, offering practical advice and sharing Scripture that had helped him during his darkest times. His words carried weight because they came from expe-rience—experience rooted in rebellion but redeemed by grace.

Watching him minister to this struggling couple re-minded me how far he had come and how powerful God's redemptive work could be through someone willing to surrender fully to His will.

As I left his office that evening, my heart swelled with gratitude for the journey Ethan had taken—a journey from near-prodigal to passionate minister and counselor for others navigating similar storms.

I sat in our living room, the air filled with a mixture of nostalgia and anticipation. John and I had called a family meeting, an event that had become rare now that the kids were grown and had families of their own. Michael, Jessica, and Ethan sat on the couch, their spouses beside them. The grandchildren played quietly in the corner, oblivious to the gravity of the moment.

John cleared his throat. "We wanted to gather you all here today because there's something important we need to share."

I reached for the wooden baton we had picked up years ago during a church retreat. It was engraved with the words "Faithful Stewardship." Holding it brought back a flood of memories—both joyous and painful—of raising our children with unwavering conviction.

"Your father and I have spent our lives trying to guide you in the ways of the Lord," I began, my voice steady but my heart pounding. "We've made mistakes, we've had battles, but through it all, our goal has always been to honor God in our family."

Michael nodded, a glimmer of understanding in his eyes. Jessica reached over to squeeze her husband's hand while Ethan watched intently, his face a mix of respect and curiosity.

John took the baton from me and held it up for everyone to see. "This represents our commitment to living out a

Christ-centered life," he said. "Today, we want to pass this baton to each of you."

He handed it first to Michael, who accepted it solemnly. "Son, you're now the head of your household. Lead with integrity and never waver from your faith."

Michael's eyes met John's, and he nodded. "I will, Dad."

Next was Jessica. John placed the baton in her hands. "Jess, you've always been strong-willed, but that strength can be a great asset in leading your family spiritually."

Tears welled up in her eyes as she accepted the baton. "Thank you," she whispered.

Finally, Ethan received it. "Ethan, you've become a pillar not just for our family but for many others. Keep standing firm in your faith."

Ethan gripped the baton firmly. "I promise," he said.

As I looked at each of my children holding that symbolic baton, I felt a weight lift off my shoulders. We were letting go of control but affirming that our parenting philosophies were rooted deeply within them.

"You're all capable of creating your own Christ-centered families," I said softly. "And though we may not always be there to guide you, remember that God is always with you."

I watched my children as they absorbed the significance of the baton. The room grew quiet, and I could sense the weight of our words settling into their hearts. It was a delicate moment, one that required a careful balance.

Later that evening, I found myself alone in the kitchen, washing dishes while my mind wrestled with a new reality. My role as the matriarch had shifted. No longer could I be the authoritarian who laid down the law. But neither could I become passive, silently watching from the sidelines.

I sighed and dried my hands, staring out the window into the dimming twilight. How could I strike the right tone between offering advice and meddling? My heart ached with the desire to continue guiding my children, but I knew that unsolicited counsel often fell on deaf ears.

"Lord," I prayed softly, "give me wisdom to know when to speak and when to stay silent."

As if in response, a memory surfaced of my own mother's gentle yet firm guidance. She never forced her opinions on me but always spoke truth when it was needed. Could I emulate that same balance? Could I be a godly, truth-speaking grandmother when called upon?

The sound of footsteps brought me back to the present. Jessica entered the kitchen, her eyes still red from earlier tears.

"Mom," she began hesitantly, "can we talk?"

"Of course," I replied, setting aside the dish towel.

She sat down at the table, fiddling with her wedding ring. "I'm struggling with how to discipline Emily. She's been so defiant lately."

I took a seat across from her, choosing my words carefully. "Jessica, parenting is never easy, and each child is different. But remember what we talked about today—upholding biblical principles while showing love."

She nodded slowly. "I want to do that, but it's hard not to let my emotions take over."

"Trust me, I understand," I said with a small smile. "But consistency is key. And always back up your discipline with love and understanding."

Jessica looked relieved, as if a burden had been lifted off her shoulders. "Thanks, Mom."

As she left the kitchen, I realized this was my new role—not as an authoritarian figure but as a supportive guide who speaks truth when needed and loves unconditionally.

As I sat in the quiet of my kitchen, memories of raising my children flooded back like a tidal wave, carrying with it both laughter and tears. Those days felt like a lifetime ago, yet some moments remained as vivid as if they had happened yesterday.

I could almost hear Michael's defiant voice echoing through the hallways. He had always been the most headstrong, constantly pushing boundaries and questioning every rule. I remembered the countless times he rolled his eyes at family devotionals, calling me a "Bible-thumper." Yet, in those rebellious eyes, I also saw glimpses of a heart wrestling with deeper truths.

Jessica's teenage years were another rollercoaster. Her insistence on wearing immodest styles led to more tearful blowups than I could count. I could still see her standing in the doorway, eyes blazing with defiance, calling me a "prude" for not allowing her to leave the house in short shorts. But beneath that rebellious exterior lay a girl searching for her identity in a confusing world.

And then there was Ethan, my youngest. His innocence made it all the harder when he began questioning his faith.

The arguments from non-believing professors shook him to his core, and I saw my diligent teachings begin to unravel before my eyes. His questions were like daggers to my heart, yet they were also an opportunity for deeper conversations and renewed faith.

I laughed softly as I recalled the chaos of trying to get all three kids up and ready for school each morning. Michael would drag his feet, Jessica would spend too long on her hair, and Ethan would always manage to spill something on his clothes. Amidst the mayhem, there was an underlying sense of love and routine that kept us grounded.

But it wasn't all chaos and conflict. There were also moments of deep joy and connection that made it all worthwhile. I remembered the family game nights filled with laughter, the bedtime stories where we would huddle together and read about heroes of faith, and the countless prayers whispered over sleeping children.

Those tough seasons bore fruit in ways that weren't apparent then. Michael now reads Bible stories to his own kids with the same fervor he once resisted. Jessica's softer approach to parenting is rooted in the principles she once rebelled against but now appreciates. And Ethan's journey from doubt to passionate ministry has inspired many others.

Reflecting on those peaks and valleys, I realized that every trial had been a stepping stone toward something greater. The laughter and tears had woven a tapestry of faith, love, and resilience that bound our family together through thick and thin.

I knelt by the side of my bed, the soft glow of the lamp casting a warm light over my Bible. My heart felt full as I thought about my grandchildren, their innocent faces and boundless energy bringing a new kind of joy to my life. I began to pray, my voice a soft whisper in the stillness of the night.

"Lord, I come before You with a heart full of gratitude and hope. Thank You for the precious gift of my grandchildren. I ask that You raise them up as mighty warriors in their time, just as You did with my own children."

My mind drifted to each of their faces—Michael's little ones, so full of curiosity and wonder; Jessica's children, already showing signs of strong-willed determination; and Ethan's young ones, tender and thoughtful. I prayed for each one by name, asking God to guide them and protect them.

"Father, grant them wisdom beyond their years. May they grow to know You deeply and love You fiercely. Let their lives be a testament to Your grace and mercy."

I paused, feeling the weight of these prophetic blessings. The responsibility I felt as their grandmother was immense, but it was also a joy. These little ones were not just the next generation—they were the future torchbearers of our family's faith.

"Lord, give them courage to stand firm in their beliefs, even when the world around them wavers. Fill them with Your Spirit so they may discern truth from falsehood and walk in Your light all the days of their lives."

As I prayed, I felt an overwhelming sense of peace. Despite all the struggles and challenges we had faced as a family, God's faithfulness had never wavered. He had been our rock, our fortress, our deliverer.

"And Father," I continued, "let me never forget that above all else, I remain their spiritual mother—now and forever. Help me to guide them with love and wisdom, to be a source of encouragement and strength."

I ended my prayer with a deep sense of fulfillment. Though my role had evolved over the years from mother to grandmother, one thing remained constant: my unwavering commitment to be a spiritual anchor for my family.

Chapter 10

Reflections and Lessons Learned

I sat on the porch, the wicker chair creaking slightly beneath me. The sun dipped low in the sky, casting long shadows over the garden. A gentle breeze rustled the leaves, carrying with it the faint scent of blooming jasmine. I wrapped my hands around my tea cup, feeling its warmth seep into my skin. It was a moment of tranquility, a rare gift in the midst of life's hustle and bustle.

As I sipped my tea, my mind began to wander, drifting back through the decades. The journey of raising my children had been long and arduous, filled with moments of joy and heartbreak, triumphs and trials. I had always known that my role as a mother was more than just about providing for their physical needs; it was about shaping their souls, guiding them towards a life rooted in faith.

I remembered those early days with Michael, Jessica, and Ethan. The sleepless nights, the tantrums, the endless questions—all of it seemed so distant now. Yet each memory was vivid, etched into my heart like a cherished photograph. I recalled the first time I had to discipline Michael, how his tears had broken my heart even as I knew it was necessary. Those moments were tough love in action, a testament to the biblical principles John and I had vowed to uphold.

My thoughts shifted to more recent years, watching my children grow into adults and start families of their own. It hadn't been easy seeing them make choices that sometimes strayed from what we had taught them. But through it all, I clung to prayer and faith, trusting that God's hand was at work even when I couldn't see it.

Now, as I sat on the porch in this serene moment of reflection, I felt a deep sense of fulfillment. The final chapters of my journey as a mother were unfolding before me, and I wanted to impart the hard-earned wisdom I'd gathered along the way.

Raising children wasn't about being their friend; it was about being their guide and anchor in a world full of shifting values. It required unwavering commitment to biblical standards, even when society pushed back. And though there had been moments of intense struggle and doubt, the fruits of those labors were now evident in the lives of my grandchildren.

I took another sip of tea and breathed deeply, allowing myself to savor this peaceful evening. There was still much to be done, many more prayers to be whispered and lessons to be shared. But for now, I simply rested in the knowledge that by God's grace, we had come this far.

As I sat on the porch, the evening's tranquility gave way to a cascade of memories, each one tinted with a hint of regret. I couldn't help but think of those times when my discipline might have crossed the line into harshness. Michael's teenage years came to mind—his eyes, filled with defiance and hurt, as I laid down the law about his video games and curfews. My heart aches remembering how I had insisted on strict adherence to rules, sometimes at the expense of our relationship.

I also recalled Jessica's tearful outbursts over her wardrobe choices. Her pleas for a bit of freedom met with my unwavering refusal to allow what I deemed immodest clothing. Those moments were fraught with tension and sorrow, and I often wonder if I could have handled them with more grace.

Ethan, my youngest, had always been more compliant, but even he bore the brunt of my unyielding standards. I remember a time when he asked innocently about watching a popular TV show all his friends were raving about. My swift denial felt like a hammer blow to his innocent curiosity.

I sighed deeply, feeling the weight of those years pressing down on me. In my fervor to uphold biblical principles, had I missed out on life moments that could have fostered deeper connections with my children? Birthday parties cut short because of Sunday morning church services, family vacations tinged with anxiety over maintaining spiritual routines—it all swirled in my mind like a tapestry woven with both bright and dark threads.

Yet, despite these regrets, one thing remained unshakable: my conviction that upholding God's standards was paramount. Society's shifting values and permissive attitudes never swayed me from what I believed was right for my family. And while there were moments I wished I could change—softening my approach or choosing words more carefully—I knew in my heart that compromising on those convictions would have been far worse.

I took another sip of tea, letting its warmth soothe me. It was true that the journey had been fraught with difficult choices and emotional turmoil. But as I looked out at the garden, now bathed in the soft glow of twilight, I felt a sense of peace. The principles John and I had instilled in our children were now bearing fruit in their own families.

In the end, while I might wish for some do-overs, I found solace in knowing that through it all, we had stayed true to our faith. And that was something I'd never regret.

The toll that our parenting style took on my marriage to John was significant, though not immediately evident. In the beginning, we were united in our convictions, fervently discussing how to raise our children with a strong spiritual foundation. Yet, as the years went by and the children's defiance grew more pronounced, cracks began to appear.

There were nights when I lay in bed, staring at the ceiling, feeling utterly unsupported. John's more lenient approach often clashed with my strict discipline. He would say things like, "Sarah, maybe we should ease up a bit. They need some room to breathe." His words felt like daggers at times, undermining the rigorous standards I believed were non-negotiable.

One particularly tense evening, after another heated argument with Michael over his video games, John pulled me aside. "Sarah," he said, his voice tinged with frustration, "we're losing them. Can't you see that? Maybe if we backed off a little..."

I felt a surge of anger and betrayal. "Back off? You think being their friend is going to solve everything?" My voice trembled as I spoke.

His face softened, but his eyes held firm. "I just think there's a middle ground we're missing."

That night, we argued until the early hours, our whispered voices escalating into hushed shouts so as not to wake the children. The disagreement left me feeling isolated and questioning if our united front was cracking under pressure.

But even in those moments of tension and disagreement, there were times when our bond grew stronger. After particularly challenging days, we would retreat to our room and pray together. Those quiet moments of shared faith helped bridge the gap between us.

One such night stands out vividly in my memory. We had just dealt with a particularly severe incident involving Jessica sneaking out to meet her boyfriend. Exhausted and emotionally drained, I sat on the edge of our bed, tears streaming down my face.

John sat beside me and took my hand in his. "We'll get through this," he said softly. "Together."

His words weren't a magical solution to our problems, but they reminded me that I wasn't alone in this struggle. Over time, these moments of unity became more frequent. We learned to balance each other out—my firmness tempered by his compassion.

Ultimately, it was our shared faith that kept us grounded. Even when we disagreed on the methods, we never lost sight of the end goal: raising children who knew and loved God. In that mission, we remained steadfast partners.

Being constantly questioned and challenged took a psychological toll I hadn't anticipated. Every confrontation with Michael, Jessica, or Ethan left me second-guessing myself. Was I too harsh? Too lenient? The doubt gnawed at me during my loneliest moments, creeping into my mind even in the early hours of the morning when I should have been resting. I would lie awake, replaying every argument, every word exchanged, wondering if I had failed them in some fundamental way. The weight of responsibility felt heavier with each passing day, and I began to doubt not just my parenting, but my very ability to guide them through the tumultuous paths they were each navigating.

I remember one night vividly. Michael had stormed out after another argument about his curfew. The door slammed shut, leaving an echo that reverberated through my heart. I sat in the living room, staring at the family photo on the mantel, wondering if I was failing as a mother. The room felt colder, the silence oppressive as I tried to collect my thoughts.

The self-doubt crept in like a thief in the night. What if I was pushing them away rather than guiding them toward righteousness? What if my strict rules were building walls instead of bridges? I could hear Jessica's voice in my head, challenging my decisions, questioning my authority, and Ethan's quiet rebellion, his silent defiance more piercing than any shouted words. Their faces in the photograph seemed to mock my efforts, each smile a reminder of simpler times when love and discipline felt more straightforward. My heart ached with the weight of my uncertainty, and I prayed for wisdom, for the strength to be the mother they needed, even if I couldn't always be the mother they wanted.

In those heartbroken lows, it was my faith that pulled me through. I would retreat to my prayer closet, a small room off the bedroom filled with scriptures taped to the walls and a worn-out kneeling cushion. There, in the stillness, I poured out my anguish to God.

"Lord," I would whisper through tears, "am I doing this right? Am I leading them astray?"

Sometimes, there were no immediate answers—just the quiet reassurance of His presence that wrapped around me like a comforting embrace. Other times, a scripture would come to mind, offering solace and guidance, like a beacon in the fog. "Train up a child in the way he should go: and when he is old, he will not depart from it" (Proverbs 22:6). Those words became my lifeline, a steadying force amidst the chaos of parenting. They reminded me that even though Michael had strayed and Jessica had resisted, and Ethan had his rebellious moments, there was hope. Each of their journeys, no matter how tumultuous, was part of a greater plan.

Godly mentors also played an indispensable role during these trying times. My pastor's wife, Miriam, had walked similar paths with her own children. Over countless cups of tea at her kitchen table, she listened without judgment.

"Sarah," she'd say gently, "you're planting seeds. It may take time to see the fruit, but trust that God is working in their hearts."

Her wisdom provided much-needed perspective and reminded me that motherhood wasn't about immediate results but long-term faithfulness.

There were also older women at church who shared their stories of wayward children finding their way back. Their testimonies were beacons of hope amidst my stormy seas of doubt.

In those conversations and prayers, I found strength to continue. Though questioned and challenged constantly, these moments of faith and mentorship renewed my resolve to stay the course—to be not just their friend but their spiritual mother first and foremost.

Every morning, I started my day with a routine that had become as essential to me as breathing. My Bible sat on the kitchen table, its pages worn and marked with years of notes and prayers. Before the house woke, before the chaos of getting three kids ready for school began, I would sit in the dim light with a cup of coffee and my devotional. This was my sacred time, a moment of peace to center myself in God's word.

I'd read a passage, often returning to my favorite Psalms, letting the words wash over me. Psalm 23 was a constant companion: "The Lord is my shepherd; I shall not want." Its promise of guidance and provision gave me strength. After reading, I'd spend time in prayer, laying all my worries at His feet.

"Lord, give me wisdom today," I'd pray earnestly, my heart heavy with the weight of my responsibilities. "Help me to lead Michael, Jessica, and Ethan in Your ways. Grant me patience and understanding as I navigate the challenges each child brings, from Michael's rediscovered faith, to Jessica's spirited independence, to Ethan's evolving journey. Guide me in being a source of love and strength for them."

These extended prayer times were more than just petitions; they were conversations with my Heavenly Father. I poured out my fears, my hopes, my gratitude. There were days when I felt too overwhelmed to find the right words, so I'd sit in silence, trusting that He knew the depths of my heart.

Scripture memorization became another anchor for me. Throughout the day, when faced with challenges or moments of doubt, I'd recall verses committed to memory. Proverbs 3:5-6 was a lifeline: "Trust in the Lord with all your heart and lean not on your own understanding; in all your ways submit to Him, and He will make your paths straight." Repeating these truths reminded me that I wasn't alone in this journey.

Our local church community played an indispensable role in supporting our family. Sunday services were non-negotiable for us—a time to worship together, hear God's word preached powerfully by Pastor James, and be rejuvenated for the week ahead. The fellowship we experienced there was a lifeline.

After services, we often stayed for potlucks or small group meetings where we connected with other families facing similar challenges. Sharing our struggles and victories in these gatherings fostered a sense of solidarity and encouragement. The church wasn't just a place we attended; it was an extension of our family.

Miriam's kitchen table talks provided wisdom beyond measure. The older women's stories were testaments of God's faithfulness through every trial. And when things got especially tough at home, knowing we had people praying for us provided an immeasurable comfort.

In these disciplines—daily devotionals, extended prayers, scripture memorization—and through the unwavering support of our church community, I found the strength to continue leading my children toward God's truth amidst life's many storms.

Owning up to the role of constant rule-enforcer was one of the most challenging aspects of my journey as a mother. No loving mother wants to be seen as the bad guy, the one who constantly lays down the law and enforces boundaries. I would often catch a glimpse of myself in the mirror and wonder if my children saw me as just a stern face, a disciplinarian devoid of warmth.

There were countless moments when I longed to simply be their friend, to laugh freely without worrying about the moral implications of every joke or activity. I yearned to indulge their whims and let them have the freedoms their friends enjoyed without a second thought. But deep down, I knew that was not my calling. The weight of responsibility pressed heavily on my shoulders, a cross I had to bear out of love.

I remember vividly the day Jessica came downstairs in an outfit that made my heart sink—a crop top and shorts that left little to the imagination. Her face was defiant, ready for battle. "Jessica," I started, taking a deep breath to steady myself, "you know we have standards in this house about modesty."

"Why do you always have to ruin everything?" she shot back, her eyes flashing with anger. "All my friends get to wear what they want! You're such a prude!"

Her words stung more than she could ever know. It wasn't just about the clothes; it was about the deeper issue of guiding her heart toward purity and self-respect. "Jessica," I said softly but firmly, "this isn't about ruining your fun. It's about teaching you to value yourself in a way that honors God."

Her eyes rolled, and she stormed back upstairs, slamming her door with a force that shook the house. Moments like these left me feeling like an island—isolated, misunderstood, often resented.

But each night as I knelt beside my bed, pouring out my heart in prayer, I felt a sense of conviction wash over me. Being a mother who upholds biblical standards meant carrying burdens that weren't always appreciated in the moment. It meant enduring eye rolls, slammed doors, and harsh words because I loved my children enough to guide them toward God's truth.

This conviction didn't make the role any easier or less lonely. But it did give me peace knowing that my efforts were not in vain.

As I look back on the years of raising my children, I can clearly see the philosophy behind my parenting tough love approach. It was never about controlling their lives or stifling their individuality. It was about setting boundaries that would ultimately strengthen their character and prepare them for a world that doesn't always offer second chances.

I remember one particularly trying episode with Michael. He had come home late, well past his curfew, smelling faintly of smoke. My heart raced with a mix of anger and fear as I confronted him in the hallway.

"Michael, you know the rules. Curfew is at ten, not midnight," I said, my voice steady but firm.

He shrugged nonchalantly, "Mom, it's just a couple of hours. No big deal."

"No big deal?" I echoed, feeling the weight of this teachable moment. "When we set boundaries, they're there for a reason. You broke our trust tonight."

The consequence was immediate and clear: he lost his driving privileges for a month. It wasn't just about punishment; it was about teaching him responsibility and accountability. Michael protested vehemently, calling me unreasonable and out of touch. But deep inside, I knew this was a lesson he needed to learn now, rather than later when the stakes could be much higher.

Then there was Jessica and her insistence on attending parties where I knew alcohol flowed freely among underage kids. The arguments were fierce and frequent.

"Everyone else is going! Why do you have to be so strict?" she would plead, her eyes filled with frustration.

"Because I love you enough to say no," I would respond quietly but resolutely. "I'm not here to be your friend; I'm here to guide you toward what's right."

Allowing her to attend those parties without any oversight would have been easier in the short term—no arguments, no tears—but it would have compromised her safety and integrity. Upholding these boundaries often made me wildly unpopular with my own children, but that was a cost I was willing to bear.

And then there were the hard lessons that came with allowing natural consequences to take their course. When Ethan failed a test because he hadn't studied despite my reminders, I resisted the urge to rescue him from the failing grade.

"Mom, can you talk to my teacher? Maybe she'll let me retake it," he asked hopefully.

"No, Ethan," I replied gently but firmly. "You need to learn that actions have consequences."

These experiences weren't easy for any of us. They often led to tearful nights and feelings of isolation on my part as well as theirs. But each boundary set, each consequence upheld, served as another brick in the foundation of their character.

Balancing firm boundaries while still nurturing my children felt like walking a tightrope, one misstep could send everything crashing down. It was a delicate dance of discipline and affection, correction and affirmation. I knew that for every boundary I set, there had to be an equal measure of warmth and love to cushion its impact.

One morning, after a particularly heated argument with Jessica about her clothing choices, I found her sulking in her room. The tears on her cheeks cut through my heart like a knife. I took a deep breath and knocked softly on her door.

"Jess, can we talk?" I asked gently.

She looked up, her eyes filled with a mixture of anger and hurt. "What's there to talk about? You never let me do anything."

I walked in and sat beside her on the bed, taking her hand in mine. "Jessica, I know it feels like I'm being harsh, but my rules come from a place of love. I want to protect you, not control you."

She didn't respond immediately, but she didn't pull away either. That was progress.

In moments like these, it was crucial to balance the sternness with which I upheld our family's values with constant affirmations of love. Frequent words of encouragement became my lifeline in maintaining that balance. Every night before bed, regardless of how tough the day had been, I made sure to tell each of my children how much I loved them and how proud I was of their efforts.

Quality time also played a vital role in this balancing act. Despite the chaos that often filled our days, we always found time for family dinners where we'd share stories and laugh together. Sunday afternoons were reserved for baking cookies or playing board games—simple activities that created warmth and unity at home.

One evening stands out vividly in my memory. We were all gathered around the dining table for dinner. The smell of roasted chicken filled the air as we held hands to say grace.

"Lord, thank you for this meal and for each member of this family," John began. "Help us to love one another as You love us."

As we dug into our meal, Michael shared about a project he was excited about at school, Jessica talked about a new book she was reading, and Ethan made us all laugh with his impressions of his teachers.

In those moments, it was clear that the strict standards we upheld were understood by my children as being rooted in love, not coldness. The boundaries were there not to stifle them but to guide them toward becoming the best versions of themselves. Through quality time and constant affirmations, they saw beyond the rules to the heart behind them—a heart deeply committed to their well-being and spiritual growth.

This tightrope walk required constant vigilance and adjustment. It wasn't perfect; there were stumbles along the way. But in weaving discipline with affection, firmness with warmth, I aimed to create an environment where my children felt both loved unconditionally and guided unwaveringly toward what was right.

Looking back over the years, I often find myself reflecting on the many battles we fought and the tears we shed. Raising children in today's world demands a resilience and steadfastness that can be both exhausting and heart-wrenching. For any new parents reading this, I want to offer some hard-earned advice.

First, know that the inevitable blowback you will face is worth enduring. When you choose to uphold strong values and set firm boundaries, there will be resistance. Your children may lash out, call you names, or accuse you of being unfair. They might even say they hate you in moments of anger. But remember this: their anger is often a sign that they need those boundaries, even if they can't see it at the time.

I vividly recall a moment when Michael stormed into his room, slamming the door so hard it rattled the pictures on the wall. He was furious because I had forbidden him from attending a party where there would be no supervision. At that moment, it felt like my heart was breaking. The temptation to give in just to restore peace was overwhelming. But I stood firm because I knew my responsibility was to guide him, not to be his friend.

Encourage your children with love but remain uncompromising in your standards. It's a tough balance, but one that's essential for their growth and well-being. There will be times when this stance makes you deeply unpopular with your kids and perhaps even with other parents or society at large. But don't let popularity sway you from what you know is right.

Jessica once called me a "prude" during one of our many arguments about her clothing choices. It stung, but I held my ground because I believed it was my duty to protect her dignity and self-respect. Those moments of unpopularity were difficult, but looking back, they were pivotal in shaping her character.

Your role as a parent is not to seek approval but to raise your children with unwavering love and standards. The path may be fraught with conflict and doubt, but trust that enduring these trials will ultimately mold them into individuals of integrity and faith.

Stay strong in your convictions, new parents. The blowback is temporary, but the impact of your steadfast love and guidance will last a lifetime.

Sitting on the porch with a cup of tea in my hand, I often find myself reflecting on the many sleepless nights and the turmoil that seemed endless at the time. I remember the heated arguments, the tearful confrontations, and the countless hours spent in fervent prayer. But now, as I watch my children live out their faith and raise godly grandchildren, I see that every moment of struggle was worth it.

Michael, who once seemed so determined to rebel against everything John and I stood for, is now a devoted husband and father. He reads Bible stories to his own children just as I did with him. Seeing him kneel by their bedside, leading them in prayer, fills my heart with indescribable joy. It's a testament to the seeds planted during those tumultuous years.

Jessica, despite her rebellious streak, has embraced her faith in ways I once feared she never would. She may have adopted a more permissive style with her children, but she remains rooted in the values we instilled. Watching her guide her children with love and patience reassures me that the foundation we built has not crumbled.

Ethan's transformation from near-prodigal to passionate minister is nothing short of miraculous. His dedication to mentoring youth and upholding Biblical standards echoes the principles we fought so hard to instill in him. When I see him counseling struggling parents or passionately preaching about God's love and discipline, I know that our efforts were not in vain.

The joy of knowing that I played a part in forging unshakable testimonies and legacies is overwhelming. Each time one of my grandchildren quotes Scripture or speaks about their faith with conviction, it feels like a small victory—a confirmation that the battles fought were for a greater purpose.

As I watch them grow, I'm reminded that the sleepless nights and heartaches were but fleeting moments compared to the lasting impact of raising children who walk in faith. Every prayer whispered, every boundary enforced, every tear shed has borne fruit in ways I couldn't have imagined at the time.

In these quiet moments of reflection, surrounded by reminders of God's grace and faithfulness, I'm filled with a deep sense of peace and gratitude. The journey was arduous, but seeing my children thrive in their faith and pass those values down to their own families makes it all worthwhile.

Chapter 11

The Cherished Inheritance

The church was abuzz with anticipation as family and friends gathered for a significant milestone: my granddaughter Lily's baby dedication. The sunlight filtered through the stained glass windows, casting colorful patterns on the pews. The scent of fresh flowers mingled with the faint aroma of polished wood, creating an atmosphere both sacred and serene.

I sat in the front row, holding John's hand, my heart swelling with a mix of pride and gratitude. Michael stood at the altar with his wife, Emily, cradling Lily in his arms. They had chosen to dedicate her life to God in a ceremony that mirrored the one we had for Michael all those years ago. It was a full-circle moment that underscored the spiritual legacy we had fought so hard to establish.

Pastor Williams, a long-time family friend, began the ceremony with a heartfelt prayer. His voice resonated through the sanctuary, a familiar comfort that brought tears to my eyes. "Lord, we thank You for this precious gift of life," he intoned, "and we ask for Your guidance and blessing over Lily as she grows."

Michael stepped forward, his voice steady yet emotional as he recited Proverbs 31:25-28:

"Strength and honor are her clothing;
She shall rejoice in time to come.
She opens her mouth with wisdom,
And on her tongue is the law of kindness.
She watches over the ways of her household,
And does not eat the bread of idleness.
Her children rise up and call her blessed."

His words hung in the air like a benediction, echoing the values we had instilled in him. As he spoke, I saw not just my son but a man who had embraced his role as a spiritual leader in his own family. It was a poignant reminder of the power of faith and dedication.

After the reading, Pastor Williams gently took Lily into his arms. He anointed her forehead with oil and offered a blessing that resonated deeply within me. "May she grow in wisdom and stature," he prayed, "and may her life be a testament to God's enduring love."

The congregation responded with a heartfelt "Amen," and I couldn't help but smile through my tears. The ceremony concluded with a hymn that we all sang together, our voices blending into a harmonious tribute to God's faithfulness.

As we exited the church and gathered for photos outside, I looked at my family—three generations bound by faith and love. This moment wasn't just about Lily; it was about the enduring legacy of spiritual commitment that would guide her throughout her life.

I stood there, taking in the sight of my children and grandchildren gathered around. The sun shone brightly, illuminating their faces with a golden hue. Michael, holding Lily, had a serene smile that spoke volumes of his contentment. It felt like just yesterday I held him for the first time, promising to raise him in God's ways.

I remembered Michael's teenage years vividly—the sarcasm, the defiance, the nights spent in prayer hoping he would find his way back. Those years were tough, marked by heated arguments and a few broken hearts. But then came the breakthrough. One evening, after a particularly fiery argument about his choice of friends, he came to me with tears in his eyes and asked for guidance. That was the turning point. He began to attend youth group earnestly, read Scripture on his own, and even started mentoring younger kids.

Jessica stood nearby, chatting animatedly with her cousin. Her rebellious teenage phase had been a whirlwind of immodest clothing choices and poor decisions in friends. I remembered the countless times we clashed over her outfits and behavior. There was one night when she screamed that I was ruining her life by being so strict. It broke my heart, but I knew I had to stand firm. The breakthrough with Jessica came unexpectedly during a youth retreat. She returned home with a renewed spirit and a softer heart. She apologized for the hurtful things she'd said and started taking her faith seriously.

Ethan was chasing after one of his nephews, laughing as they played tag. He had always been the most tender-hearted of my children but went through a crisis of faith during college that nearly broke me. His professors filled his mind with skepticism, and he began questioning everything we had taught him. There were sleepless nights filled with tearful prayers for his return to faith. His spiritual breakthrough came during a mission trip he reluctantly joined. He saw firsthand the power of God's love in action and returned home transformed.

Each journey was fraught with challenges but also marked by moments of profound spiritual awakening that reaffirmed my commitment to raising them in the faith. Seeing them now—strong, faithful adults—filled me with a deep sense of gratitude.

As I watched them interact with their children, teaching them Bible verses or sharing stories from Scripture, I knew every hardship had been worth it.

I stood in front of the mantle, gazing at the collection of family portraits that spanned decades. Each frame held a story, a memory etched in time.

The earliest ones took me back to when my children were just little. There was Michael, not more than five, grinning with a toothy smile while holding a Bible nearly half his size. Jessica, with her pigtails and missing front teeth, stood next to him holding her favorite doll. Ethan, the baby then, sat on my lap with wide, curious eyes that seemed to take in everything around him. John stood behind us, his hand resting protectively on my shoulder. Those were simpler times when the biggest challenge was getting them to sit still for the camera.

As the years passed, the portraits changed. I remember one Christmas card photo vividly. The kids were in their awkward pre-teen years—Michael with braces, Jessica experimenting with bangs, and Ethan clutching a soccer ball. We stood in front of our modest Christmas tree, adorned with handmade ornaments and twinkling lights. Despite the chaos that often came with those years, their smiles shone brightly.

Then came the period when each child started finding their path. In one portrait, Michael had just graduated high school. He stood tall in his cap and gown, a symbol of the journey ahead. Jessica wore her first prom dress, looking every bit the young lady she was becoming. Ethan was in his early teens then, already showing signs of the thoughtful man he would grow into.

The most recent portraits captured our growing family. The first one included Michael's wife, Lily—a beautiful addition who brought joy and balance to our family dynamics. Jessica's husband, Daniel, stood beside her with an arm wrapped lovingly around her waist. Ethan's fiancée, Grace, joined us for one of these pictures just before their wedding.

And then there were the grandkids—each a new chapter in our family's story. Christmas cards now featured little ones with wide-eyed wonder as they experienced their first snowfall or opened gifts under the tree. One particular photo held a special place in my heart: all of us gathered around a table for Thanksgiving, three generations united by faith and love.

These portraits told a story of growth and grace through trials and triumphs. They were more than just pictures; they were milestones of God's faithfulness in our lives. As I looked at them now, I felt an overwhelming sense of gratitude for each moment captured in time.

I gathered my children in the living room, a place that had witnessed so many of our family's pivotal moments. The atmosphere was thick with a mix of anticipation and reverence. Michael, Jessica, and Ethan stood before me, their spouses and children looking on with curiosity. It was a moment I had both longed for and dreaded—passing the torch.

"Mom," Michael began, his voice steady yet soft. "We know you have something important to share."

I took a deep breath, feeling the weight of the years settle into my bones. "Yes, Michael," I replied, looking each of them in the eyes. "It's time for me to formally pass on the spiritual leadership to you."

I held out a worn Bible, the one I had read from every night at bedtime when they were young. It was full of highlighted verses, dog-eared pages, and scribbled notes in the margins—a testament to years of seeking wisdom and guidance.

"This Bible has been our anchor," I said, my voice wavering slightly. "It's been my guide through sleepless nights, rebellious phases, and moments of joy. Now it's yours to carry forward."

Michael stepped forward first. His hands trembled slightly as he took the Bible from mine. "Mom," he said quietly, his eyes moistening. "Thank you for everything."

I turned to Jessica next. She had her own Bible now, but I placed my hands on her shoulders and looked deeply into her eyes. "Jessica," I said softly, "you've grown into a wonderful mother. Keep leading your children in faith."

Tears rolled down her cheeks as she nodded, unable to speak.

Finally, I faced Ethan. He had recently taken on a ministry role at his church, a transformation that filled me with immeasurable pride. "Ethan," I said, placing a hand over his heart. "You have such a passion for God's word. Keep that fire burning."

He pulled me into a tight hug. "I will, Mom," he whispered.

I stepped back and looked at all three of them together—my children who were now parents themselves. The torch had been passed physically with that old Bible but spiritually through years of prayers, lessons, and unwavering love.

"Remember," I said firmly but lovingly, "you are now the spiritual leaders for this next generation. Lead with grace, humility, and unwavering faith."

Their spouses gathered around them as if forming a protective circle. The room filled with an unspoken understanding—this was not just an end but a beginning for all of us.

"Go forth with my blessing," I said finally. "And always remember that God is with you."

I sat on the porch swing, my granddaughter Lily nestled beside me. The summer sun filtered through the oak trees, casting dappled shadows on the ground. She had her mother's eyes—Jessica's eyes—full of curiosity and a hint of mischief.

"Grandma," she began, her voice hesitant. "Why do you always talk about staying strong in faith? Isn't it hard?"

I smiled gently, wrapping an arm around her shoulders. "Oh, Lily, it can be very hard. But it's also one of the greatest joys."

She looked up at me, waiting for more. "You know," I continued, "there were times when your mom and uncles didn't understand why I was so strict about our faith. They thought I was just being difficult."

Lily giggled softly. "Like when Mom wasn't allowed to wear certain clothes?"

"Exactly," I said with a chuckle. "But those rules weren't just about clothes. They were about teaching respect—for oneself and for God."

Her expression grew serious. "Did it hurt when they didn't understand?"

"Yes, it did," I admitted. "It hurt a lot. But I knew that sticking to those principles was important for their growth and their relationship with God."

Lily nodded slowly, absorbing my words. "So, even when it's hard, we should still stand firm?"

"Absolutely," I affirmed. "Standing firm in your faith isn't just about following rules; it's about understanding why those rules matter. It's about knowing that God has a purpose for each of us and that staying true to Him will guide us to that purpose."

She leaned her head on my shoulder, seeking comfort and assurance. "Do you think God has a special purpose for me?"

I kissed the top of her head softly. "I know He does, Lily. You are fearfully and wonderfully made, just like it says in Psalm 139. Your faith will help you discover that purpose."

She seemed to ponder this for a moment before speaking again. "What if people make fun of me or don't understand why I believe what I believe?"

"That will happen," I said honestly. "But remember what Jesus said in John 15:18—'If the world hates you, keep in mind that it hated me first.' Your faith might make you unpopular at times, but it will also make you strong."

Lily straightened up, a newfound resolve in her eyes. "I want to be strong like you, Grandma."

"You already are," I said with pride swelling in my chest. "And you will become even stronger as you grow in your faith."

The house buzzed with laughter and chatter, the walls vibrating with the joyful noise of family. Outside, the trees blazed with autumn colors—fiery reds, vibrant oranges, and mellow yellows. The scent of roasted turkey, sweet potatoes, and freshly baked pies mingled in the air, making my mouth water.

As I looked around the dining room, I couldn't help but feel a deep sense of gratitude. The table was set with our finest china, polished silverware, and a centerpiece of pumpkins and gourds. Michael stood at the head of the table, carving the turkey with practiced precision while Jessica helped set out the side dishes. Ethan entertained his young nephews with funny faces and silly stories, eliciting giggles that warmed my heart.

"Mom," Jessica called from the kitchen, "can you bring out the cranberry sauce?"

I grabbed the dish from the counter and made my way to the table. The aroma of cinnamon and nutmeg filled my nostrils as I passed by a pumpkin pie cooling on the windowsill. Setting the cranberry sauce down, I caught Michael's eye. He smiled warmly at me—an unspoken acknowledgment of our shared journey.

"Alright everyone," John's voice boomed from his seat at the other end of the table. "Let's gather 'round for grace."

We all took our places, holding hands in a circle around the table. The warmth of my family's hands enveloped me as we bowed our heads.

"Dear Lord," John began, "we thank You for this bountiful meal and for bringing us together today. We are grateful for Your blessings and for guiding us through trials and triumphs alike."

As he prayed, I glanced around at each face—Michael's wife smiling tenderly at their young son, Jessica's daughter whispering secrets to her cousin, Ethan's eyes closed in sincere reverence. My heart swelled with an ethereal contentment seeing this spiritual heritage manifest around our table.

"Amen," John concluded, and we all echoed in unison.

The clatter of serving spoons and excited voices filled the room as everyone began to dish up their plates. Conversations crisscrossed over mashed potatoes and green bean casseroles. Michael shared a story about his latest project at work; Jessica laughed about a funny moment with her kids; Ethan discussed a recent sermon that had moved him deeply.

I sat back for a moment, taking it all in—the vibrant colors of fall reflected in our feast, the warmth of family unity, and the profound joy that came from knowing our faith had woven this tapestry together. It was more than just a meal; it was a celebration of God's enduring faithfulness across generations.

My soul sang with gratitude as I watched my children and grandchildren interact so lovingly. This was what it was all about—the culmination of years of prayer, discipline, love, and unwavering faith manifesting in this beautiful moment around our Thanksgiving table.

As we settled into our meal, John tapped his glass gently with a fork, calling for attention. The clinking sound brought a hush over the room. He stood up, looking around at our gathered family with a proud smile.

"Before we dive too deep into this feast, I think it's important we take a moment to reflect on something truly special," he began. "Each of us here has been profoundly shaped by Sarah's unwavering faith and conviction. I thought it would be meaningful for us to share how her guidance impacted us."

Michael wiped his mouth with a napkin and stood first. "I'll start," he said, glancing at me with a mix of reverence and love. "Mom, there were times during my teenage years when I felt like you were too strict, that your rules were suffocating. But now, as I raise my own children, I see the wisdom in your steadfastness."

He paused, taking a deep breath. "There was a time in college when I almost drifted away from my faith entirely. But your voice was always in the back of my mind, reminding me of the values you instilled in us. Your unflinching convictions pulled me back from the edge more times than I can count."

Michael sat down, his eyes glistening with unshed tears. Jessica stood next, her hands trembling slightly as she took a deep breath. "Mom," she began softly, "I know I was your most rebellious child. There were moments when I resented you for not letting me do what all my friends were doing. But now, as I look at my own kids, I realize you were protecting me."

She looked directly at me, her eyes filled with gratitude. "Your steadfastness was a lighthouse in my stormy seas. You didn't waver, even when it meant being unpopular with me. That unwavering love and discipline are why I stand firm in my faith today."

Jessica sat down, and Ethan rose to his feet, his usually confident demeanor replaced by something more solemn. "Mom," he said quietly, "I questioned everything you taught me during college. Professors and peers made me doubt what I'd always believed. But it was your relentless prayers and the seeds you planted that brought me back."

He took a deep breath, his voice steadying as he continued. "I remember coming home one break and finding you on your knees in prayer for us kids. That image stayed with me and eventually led me back to God's path." Ethan looked around the room before meeting my eyes again. "You gave us an eternal inheritance that no earthly treasure could match."

As Ethan sat down, I felt an overwhelming sense of fulfillment wash over me. My heart swelled with gratitude as I looked at each of them—my children who had grown into faithful adults despite all the challenges along the way.

As I sit here with my journal, the house is quiet, the only sound the ticking of the grandfather clock in the hallway. It's strange, this stillness, after so many years of chaos and noise. My mind drifts back over the decades of parenting, and I feel a profound sense of gratitude mixed with a touch of melancholy.

To whoever reads these words, know that I was far from perfect. I made countless mistakes, questioned myself more times than I can remember, and often felt the weight of my decisions pressing down on me. But through it all, I aimed to be a steadfast example of God's unwavering love.

I was not your friend; I was your mother. And that made all the difference.

In those moments when my children challenged me, when they pushed against the boundaries I set, it wasn't easy to stand firm. Popular culture screamed for me to be lenient, to be their friend rather than their guide. But I knew deep down that my role required something much more profound. Friendship is fleeting; true spiritual guidance is eternal.

I remember vividly those sleepless nights spent in prayer, pleading with God for wisdom and strength. The world outside our home often felt like a storm, battering against our walls with temptations and false promises. Yet inside, I strove to create a sanctuary grounded in faith and love.

Looking back now, I see the fruits of those labors. My children have grown into adults who carry forward the values instilled in them. They are raising their own families with those same principles, passing down a legacy that started long before them and will continue long after.

To anyone who finds themselves in a similar journey—feeling overwhelmed by the enormity of parenting while trying to uphold Godly principles—take heart. The road is not easy; it's fraught with challenges and heartache. But it is worth every tear, every prayer, every moment of doubt.

Remember that you are not just shaping behaviors; you are molding souls for eternity. And while friendship with your children may seem appealing in the short term, being their steadfast guide will bear far greater fruit in the long run.

I was not your friend; I was your mother. And that made all the difference.

As I take my final breath, a gentle warmth envelops me, and the weariness of years slips away. The room around me fades, replaced by a brilliant light that draws me in. I find myself standing at the threshold of heaven, a place more beautiful than I could have ever imagined.

Golden light dances across fields of flowers that stretch endlessly, each petal glistening as if kissed by morning dew. A river of crystal-clear water flows nearby, its gentle babbling like a hymn of praise. The air is filled with a sense of peace so profound it brings tears to my eyes.

Suddenly, familiar faces emerge from the light, loved ones who had gone before me. My parents are there, their smiles radiant as they step forward to embrace me. They look exactly as I remembered them in their prime, glowing with health and joy.

"Well done, good and faithful servant," my father whispers, his voice filled with pride.

My mother's eyes sparkle with tears of joy as she holds my hands. "You've run the race well, Sarah," she says softly.

I look around and see others—friends and mentors who had been pillars of faith in my life. Their presence fills me with overwhelming gratitude and love. They all echo the same words: "Well done, good and faithful servant."

I see my beloved John, standing strong and youthful once more. His eyes meet mine with a love that has only deepened through our shared journey. He steps forward and wraps his arms around me in an embrace that feels like home.

As I pull back to look into his eyes, he smiles warmly. "We've made it," he says simply.

Beyond them all stands the One I have longed to see face to face—my Lord and Savior. His eyes are filled with such love and compassion that it takes my breath away. He steps forward and places His hand gently on my shoulder.

"Well done, good and faithful servant," He says, His voice resonating with authority and grace.

In that moment, all the struggles and heartaches of life melt away, replaced by an indescribable joy and peace. I realize that this is my final cherished inheritance—life eternal with my Lord.

Surrounded by those who modeled Christ's love for me throughout my earthly journey, I know now that every trial was worth it. I am home at last.

Epilogue

As I sit on my porch on this quiet Sunday evening, watching the sun paint the sky in shades of pink and gold, I find myself reflecting on the journey that has brought me here. The swing beneath me creaks softly—the same swing where I once rocked my babies, wiped tears, and later had heart-to-heart conversations with my teenagers. Now it holds me and occasionally my grandchildren, a testament to time's swift passage.

My children are grown now, with families of their own. Each Sunday after church, they gather here for dinner, filling my home with the beautiful chaos of little feet and children's laughter. I watch them parent their own children, and sometimes I catch glimpses of myself in their words and actions. Michael's firm but gentle correction of his son's behavior. Jessica's insistence on morning devotions with her daughters. Ethan's patient explanations of Scripture to his curious children.

They've each found their own way of passing on the faith we built together. They don't parent exactly as I did—and perhaps that's for the best. They've taken the foundation we laid and built upon it with their own understanding and the wisdom God has given them for this generation.

Sometimes, when my grandchildren ask me to tell stories about when their parents were young, I see the legacy of our journey in their wide-eyed responses. "Really, Grandma? Daddy used to get in trouble too?" they ask, giggling at tales of their father's teenage rebellion. These moments remind me that our struggles weren't just challenges to overcome—they were part of a bigger story God was writing.

The world hasn't gotten any easier for Christian parents. If anything, the challenges have grown more complex. But I see my children navigating these waters with grace and wisdom, standing firm in their faith while showing Christ's love to a world that desperately needs it.

Looking back, I understand now more than ever why being their mother—not their friend—was so crucial. Friendship is beautiful, and I cherish the deep friendship I now share with my adult children. But it was the foundation of unwavering love, consistent discipline, and steadfast faith that made that friendship possible.

To those still in the trenches of raising children in today's world: take heart. The tears you shed in prayer, the battles you fight to uphold godly principles, the moments when you feel alone in your convictions—they are not in vain. You are not just raising children; you are raising future parents, future leaders, future disciples of Christ.

The baton of faith gets passed from generation to generation, not like a pristine trophy that sits on a shelf, but like a well-worn family Bible—marked up with life's lessons, tear-stained from life's struggles, yet containing eternal truths that guide us home.

As the sun sets on another Sunday evening, I bow my head in gratitude. The journey hasn't been easy, but it has been faithful. God's promises have proven true. The seeds planted in tears have indeed borne fruit with joy.

I was not their friend; I was their mother.

And that has made all the difference—not just for one generation, but for generations to come.

The End

About the author

B orn and raised in Washington, D.C., I grew up surrounded by the country's capital's vibrant culture
and diverse communities. My teenage years were spent in
Maryland, where I sincerely appreciated the unique blend
of urban and suburban life. From a young age, I was known
for my shy and quiet demeanor, often finding solace in my
thoughts and observations. This reflective nature led me
to develop a keen interest in people, particularly in the
wisdom and experiences of older adults. I spent countless
hours in the company of elders, listening to their stories
and learning from their perspectives. This early exposure
to intergenerational interactions instilled in me a profound
respect for the lessons that can be understood by those
who have lived through different times. My journey took
a significant turn when I joined the Army and served in

Desert Storm. The experiences I gained during my military service were transformative, teaching me about resilience, teamwork, and the complexities of human nature. The discipline and perspective I acquired in the Army have been invaluable in shaping my worldview and approach to writing.

www.ingramcontent.com/pod-product-compliance
Lightning Source LLC
Chambersburg PA
CBHW050943120626
46552CB00001B/352